Breaking From the Enemy
by J.R. Sharp

ISBN 978-1-63393-699-7

Published by

◤ köehlerbooks™

210 60th Street
Virginia Beach, VA 23451
212-574-7939
www.koehlerbooks.com

Breaking From the Enemy

J. R. Sharp

VIRGINIA BEACH
CAPE CHARLES

Dedication

This book is dedicated to Gino Cartelli and all the Italian freedom fighters who risked their lives during the German occupation of Italy during World War II.

Table of Contents

Author's Note

THE STORIES MY GRANDFATHER, Gino Cartelli, and great uncle, Chester Zucchet, shared with me about surviving World War II were fascinating. I don't know if they were true, but the scars on their bodies were deep and wide. My grandfather's wounds were brutal, covering most of his body. He walked with only a slight limp, but with pride only a war hero could display.

Gino's time as an Italian freedom fighter was especially fascinating. The older I grew, the more vivid his stories became. I was proud of his actions and those of so many other Italians who knew taking up arms with Germany was a mistake.

I wrote this book based on their accounts of the war. It is also based on my extensive research into what the Nazis did to Italy and its citizens during the German occupation. Most of this book is fictional; however, most of the accounts of Gino's location and timeframes are true. Due to the lack of verifiable facts, I had to intuit what happened. The family names are real, but all other names and characters are fictional.

This is the first book in a trilogy about Gino and his time as an Italian freedom fighter. My debut book, *Feeding the Enemy*, tells the story of how my mother's family, the Zucchets, survived the horrors of World War II. The family had to grow food for the Germans and Fascists, which in itself was horrible, but they were also traumatized by their enemies' frequent visits to the farm.

Breaking From the Enemy focuses on Gino after he leaves his wife in Treviso, Italy. The story highlights his journey from Italian Royal Army soldier to Italian freedom fighter, defying the Nazi soldiers who invaded Italy.

Chapter 1

DUST FROM THE TROOP transport caravan wafted into the truck carrying Private Gino Cartelli. He shared a wooden seat with other wounded soldiers, his head hanging from the physical exhaustion and mental fatigue of traveling in the cold, open military wagon. This military convoy was headed down Italy's west coast for further service in the Italian Royal Army, which was going back to war with an ally he hated. The Nazi Germans were savages and Gino was certain they were headed toward more madness. He needed to find a way out of this war or else face certain death like so much of his family.

In the last month, he learned his two brothers were killed by the same German army he was about to rejoin forces with. The love of his life, Catherina Zucchet, was on her way home to Cimpello, her own survival uncertain. She was the reason he was still alive after taking care of him at the military hospital in Treviso.

He had been shot in the chest while working to expand electricity in Ethiopia and eventually lost one of his lungs from the injury. To make matters worse, while he was being evacuated back to Italy he contracted malaria, which almost put him underground at the tender age of twenty-seven.

As Gino continued to look out the back of the transport,

all he could see was swirling dust stirred by the truck convoy pushing through the countryside. His thoughts drifted back to the beginning of this madness, memories that now seemed like distant dreams of a better life.

Gino and his best friend, Chester Zucchet, had enlisted in the Italian Royal Army in 1938. They were both from Cimpello, just outside the city of Pordenone. Italy was in a deep depression and fighting for Benito Mussolini's ideology of Italian expansion as a way to pull the country from the doldrums. Neither Gino nor Chester wanted a life as a destitute farmer. The promise of fortunes and adventures to foreign lands lured them to wear Italy's uniform. After a short training cycle, they were both sent to Ethiopia to fight for their nation's expansion. That was two years earlier, and now Gino realized it was the biggest mistake of his life.

Italy was on a path of destruction in 1940. Benito Mussolini made some questionable decisions, and for the first time even his troops questioned the dictator's ability to lead their country. The Germans were sweeping through Europe and putting pressure on Italy to enter World War II, but Mussolini resisted because his army was already stretched too thin. He needed more troops to expand the Italian Empire, but his main problem wasn't troops—it was tanks, airplanes, and equipment. Italy didn't have the industrial might of Germany, and it was immediately apparent that the boot-shaped peninsula could easily be overrun by Hitler or other armies resisting Italy's expansionist march. Mussolini needed Hitler's war might, so he allowed the madman to pillage Italy.

The Germans treated Italy more as a conquered nation than a partner. And, for four long years, the Italian people would be abused, murdered, and plundered. Most Italian companies were converted to wartime production, and any resources, such as food, were taken to supply German troops. Mussolini feared that if he could not keep up with his Axis allies' demands, he would be left out of the spoils of the war that Germany had, so far, successfully waged through Northern Europe. Germany had sacked Denmark, Norway, Luxemburg, Poland and the Netherlands. Belgium and France would undoubtedly be next.

With each stop, the convoy of trucks grew heavier with

soldiers. Many were more beleaguered than Gino, some barely able to walk. As his countrymen boarded, Gino wondered about the next step in his military career. He hated the Nazis and the cold was unbearable. During the night, they seemed to waste hours looking for a place to stay and eat. With only one meal a day and little protection from the weather, Gino and his fellow soldiers weakened. Most of the soldiers were submissive and emaciated, but a few became openly rebellious. Gino could see that things were going to get interesting as they continued their journey south. Many of the soldiers talked about how Italy was on the wrong side of the great European war.

As he looked out of the back of the truck, he could see the decimated countryside pass by. Most of it was barren and gray; they would travel for hours before seeing anybody or anything. It was nothing like his home of Cimpello.

Gino often drifted to memories of his hospital stay and how wonderful it was to see Catherina every day. Gino knew whenever she was at the hospital because she always stopped to talk to the nurses before coming to his room. Her voice was so sweet he could pick it out in the largest of crowds. Even back in the days before the war, when they were in school and would meet at the dance hall in downtown Cimpello, he always heard her before seeing her.

His thoughts drifted to how to support his new wife when he got back from the war. Farming wasn't what he wanted to do. In fact, he disliked it even more than his father did. The army taught him all about electricity, and he could use those skills to find work when his army tour was completed. Gino wondered how his father was doing back on the family farm.

***

Gino lost track of how long they had been traveling since they left Treviso, but his best guess was five days. They stayed at a soccer stadium for the night, and it wasn't as bad as the previous night; they even had hot bread with pasta. As they were getting ready to leave the stadium, he hurried to the trucks for loading. Getting on the transport first was his priority, and Gino was lucky enough to get a seat in the front of the truck, which was warmer than the back. He started a conversation with the soldier he had dinner with the previous night. Joseph was from Venice, which was about an hour from Cimpello. This made for an instant connection. Both soldiers were concerned with what was next for their lives. Both of them wanted to get back home and decided to try for medical discharges.

As the trucks left the stadium, Gino asked Joseph if he found out anything new about the war. Joseph blew warm air into his hands and moved his legs up and down to stay warm.

"So far as I can tell from talking to the other soldiers, Italy is getting ready to invade the same countries as Germany."

Gino looked around and nodded. "Yes, that's the same thing I'm hearing, and that's why they're gathering up all of the wounded soldiers to boost the army's numbers. I also talked with a medic last night, and we're supposed to be checked out again by another doctor to see if we're fit for further service when we arrive in Naples."

Joseph's wounds were not as serious as Gino's, but he looked worse. He had been wounded in the leg and arm, but still had full use of both limbs. The medic said a soldier had to lose a limb or major organ to get discharged. Gino thought he met that criteria because he'd lost his lung, but the medic shrugged when Gino asked why he wasn't rejected back in Treviso.

***

When the trucks rolled into Naples, Gino knew it was about noon because his hunger pains had started. He never was a breakfast eater, but he ate lunch religiously. The truck was extremely quiet and he couldn't see too much, but the smells of a city became apparent as they got closer to Naples. He noticed larger buildings, wider streets, more vehicles, and horses pulling trailers. The odors ranged from fresh bread to old trash. He was getting hungrier and more anxious as time went by, as did the other soldiers in the truck. The day wasn't as cold as the preceding ones; in fact, they had opened the back of the truck to let air flow through, which felt great because most of the soldiers hadn't had a decent shower in about a week.

The truck slowed and headed into a courtyard. As the truck stopped, Gino could hear some senior enlisted men and medics yell at everyone to debark. The men were then led in front of the trucks and told to get into ranks. The courtyard was behind a white building, which Gino assumed was a hospital. In front of them was a high-ranking officer with one arm and a medical doctor. The medical doctor had a different uniform and he needed a haircut. Gino smiled. Doctors and nurses didn't care about military protocol. Gino wouldn't either if he were in their profession.

"All wounded personnel reporting for further duty, sir," a sergeant said.

The senior officer returned the salute and inspected the men.

Gino saw a row of nurses and other staff in ranks to the right. On his left, cooks worked around kettles, which meant they were going to have lunch. There was a moment of silence before orders were given to the different squads. He couldn't hear what was going on and neither could Joseph, who was standing next to him.

"What are we doing?" asked Joseph.

"I have no idea, but let's follow the crowd to the food. I'm hungry."

As the order was given to fall out, they followed personnel toward the food line. They were stopped by a mean-looking senior enlisted who told them they were going the wrong way and needed to be medically evaluated again. After being pointed to the right side of the courtyard, Gino and Joseph did what they were told. The line was long, but it moved fast. The nurses asked for the soldiers' names and looked down at the table for paperwork.

When it was Gino's turn, an attractive nurse asked for his name and he replied, "Private Gino Cartelli."

She couldn't stop looking at him for the longest time; she suddenly remembered what she was supposed to do but forgot the handsome soldier's name.

"What was your name again?" asked the nurse, her face red.

He stepped in close and looked into the nurse's brown eyes with his aqua-green ones and replied, "Private Gino Cartelli at your service."

The nurse smiled and looked for his name on the charts. After about five minutes and a discussion with the nurses on the other side of the table, the nurse came back. She asked him to step to the right and let the other soldiers go ahead of him. It soon became apparent that Gino and the other soldiers from his hospital were all being put to the right of the table. After about an hour, all the soldiers had been through the nurses' line and were headed to get lunch except for Gino's group. The beautiful nurse approached them. The older nurse accompanying her looked like she had seen every medical condition known to man.

The older nurse said, "Gentlemen, we have a problem here. It looks like we don't have any medical records on you soldiers, so we're going to have to reevaluate you here at the hospital before we can determine your next assignment. Please, fill out these forms and get something to eat."

The nurse handed out forms, with Gino being last. He stepped up as she handed him his paperwork. Grabbing her hand softly, he moved in close to her left and softly said that he needed some help filling out the paperwork. These forms could be his ticket out of the army, but he needed to write down the correct information. Who better to provide the necessary information than a nurse?

She met Gino's eyes and replied, "No problem, Private Cartelli. Come over to the table, have a seat and fill out the medical forms."

Gino did as he was told until it came to patient information on what wounds he had sustained. She was sitting next to him when he stopped writing. Grabbing the forms from him, she moved closer so nobody could hear her talk. He moved closer to her as well, but she didn't mind.

"Now, let's see where you're having problems. Looks like you're doing well except for what wounds you sustained. Private Cartelli, what wounds did you endure?" asked the nurse.

"Well, since we're talking about my wounds, you can at least give me your name."

"It's Nurse Patty, Private Cartelli. What wounds brought you here to Naples? What are we going to write in these empty places?"

Gino looked at the unfinished paperwork and switched his gaze to Patty, replying, "I was shot in the chest and had my left lung removed. In addition, I had malaria, which is still bothering me."

As Gino spoke, she recorded his answer. When she finished, she looked at Gino and remarked, "You have lost a major organ, plus had malaria. You should not be here, but I don't make that decision. The doctors will have to take another look at you. After they read what I wrote down, you will have to spend some time here before they decide what to do with you. Remember, you cannot catch your breath, you get tired easily, and for god's sake, look sick and not so handsome."

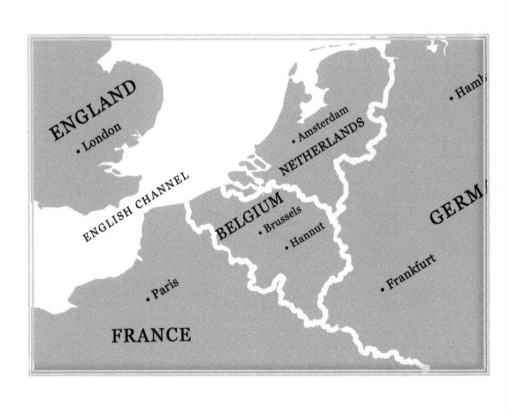

Chapter 2

IN MAY 1940, THE Germans invaded Belgium. Their strategy was to defeat Belgium and continue their march toward France. The first battle in Belgium, the Battle of Hannut, was the largest tank battle ever fought. The Germans were set to battle the French and the Allies at Hannut. The French hoped to delay the German advancement long enough to reinforce their army from other units. Fortunately for the Germans, this did not progress as planned.

The ringing in Captain Herman Schmidt's ears wasn't going away, and he was having a hard time getting back up to the turret in his tank. His head pounded with such force that even his back ached. As he reached for his turret handles, the only thing he grabbed was the air he breathed. He shook his head, but his hearing was still blunted and his vision blurry. He still wasn't clear where he was or what happened to his tank. Something dripped from his head, so he wiped what he thought was sweat but immediately noticed it was blood.

That would explain why my head hurts so much, thought the captain. After getting to his knees, his vision came back, and the first thing he realized was that he wasn't in the tank anymore. It was in front of him in a ball of flames. He looked around and noticed his German comrades rushing past him toward Hannut.

How could this have happened? he thought. *My tank was just under me and we destroyed five French tanks.* He heard plane engines above and saw the markings of the Royal Air Force (RAF) under the wings. *My tank must have been hit by a bomb, and I was thrown out of the tank, but where are the other tanks?* He tried to get to his feet, but the pain in his back prevented him from standing. He crawled to the remains of a tree trunk and lifted himself to a sitting position. All he smelled was fire, diesel fuel, and the dirt covering his uniform. More troops went by him, but he was unable to rise from his current position, no matter how hard he tried. A couple of infantry men stopped to ask him if he needed anything, but he told them to continue to the battlefield.

He closed his eyes for what seemed like only a minute, but when he opened them it was almost dusk. His beloved tank was a smoldering hunk of metal, and he heard an armored troop transport coming from the direction of the battlefield. He didn't know if it was the French or his beloved comrades from Germany, but he wasn't taking any chances. Reaching for his Luger, he pulled it out of its holster in preparation for whatever was about to happen. As the sound grew louder, he could tell it was German. He could also tell it was not coming toward him. The captain raised the Luger over his head and fired a couple shots to give his location.

The transport stopped as the commander in the front seat looked toward the shots. He saw the smoldering tank on his left, and then he heard another shot. The commander spotted two German boots and a Luger being held in the air beside a tree stump.

"Go see who is over by the tree stump," ordered the commander. The back of the transport opened and two infantry soldiers exited the vehicle.

The captain could barely hear what was going on but knew the transport had stopped. He passed out.

"It is a tank commander. He is wounded but alive," yelled one soldier.

"Load him into the transport. I'm hungry and we need to get back to our command before nightfall," ordered the commander.

One soldier grabbed the captain under his armpits while

the other grabbed the feet. As the soldiers loaded up the gravely wounded officer, the transport commander immediately noticed it was Captain Schmidt. Schmidt was a legend in the tank community, with more tank kills than any other commander. The commander put the transport in gear and moved on with the wounded captain in his care.

***

The first thing Captain Schmidt noticed was a bandage covering his eyes and wrapped around the top of his head. He could barely move without pain shooting up and down his back. If he lay perfectly flat, the pain was manageable. The aroma of battle had switched to that of clean sheets and bleach. He couldn't see, but he heard other people in the room.

"Where am I?" asked the captain.

"You are in the Berlin hospital recovering from your wounds. You should relax and let your body heal. The doctor will be in later to talk with you about your wounds," the attending nurse said.

"How long have I been here?" asked Schmidt.

"You have been here three days. Now rest."

The nurse finished her rounds and was catching up on her paperwork when the doctor entered the nurses' station.

"Has anything changed since I was here last?" asked the doctor.

"Our Captain Schmidt has come around and started talking."

The doctor grabbed his chart and reviewed it. "Well, that is good news. Did you tell him his tank career is most likely over because of his extensive back wounds?"

"No, I left that bit of good news for you," answered the nurse with a smile. The doctor smiled and picked up his charts for rounds.

The captain heard someone come into his room.

"Good morning, Captain Schmidt. How are you feeling?" asked the doctor.

"My head is pounding and my back hurts worse than my head. When can I get out of here and get back to my tank command?"

"Let's see if we can get you walking before we decide about you getting back to your command. You took shrapnel to the head and back. Let's take a look at your head and talk about your back."

The doctor removed the bandages around his head, releasing some pressure. Suddenly Schmidt felt a little better.

"You lost a lot of blood, but fortunately someone saw you and brought you back to your command. They were able to stop your bleeding before they transported you here. Looks like your head will be fine."

The captain had a hard time focusing after the bandages were removed.

"How is your vision?" asked the doctor. Schmidt blinked to focus.

"It gets better every time I blink." He reached for the top of his head but quickly removed his hand when what he touched felt like a foreign surface.

"That's where you had the shrapnel. You're lucky it didn't penetrate your skull, or you could have had brain damage. Your hair will grow back and cover the scar," remarked the doctor.

The captain moved his hand across the scar; it wasn't as bad as he first thought.

"Your back is what we need to talk about. We removed what we could, but there is still some shrapnel lodged near your spinal cord. If we remove it, there is a chance we could sever your spinal cord, which would paralyze you. If we leave the shrapnel there, any future shock to your body could move the shrapnel and cause paralysis. I am afraid the outcome is poor either way."

The captain looked at the doctor with disbelief.

"I am sorry to say, but your tank days are behind you."

The doctor closed his chart and left the room. Captain Schmidt couldn't believe what he had heard. *What am I going to do now? I must fight for my country.*

Chapter 3

IN THE SUMMER OF 1940, Germany rolled into Paris victorious. But conquering France was difficult for Germany, and the battles took a heavy toll. Hitler wanted more of Europe, so getting his wounded recovered and back to war as quickly as possible was a top priority. Hitler's focus was east, which would require an even larger army.

One of Germany's largest military hospitals was in Berlin, where most of the military wounded were shipped to recover from their wounds. Captain Herman Schmidt was on the physical therapy floor, or what he referred to as "the physical torture ward." He was on the floor doing his daily strengthening exercises. As he stretched, his mind drifted back to how far he had come in his recovery. It was slow at first, due to the pain and swelling in his back. He was in traction and heavily medicated for weeks to reduce the swelling. Not to mention he had to go through an agonizing bout of withdrawal from not getting his daily dosage of *Panzerschokolade*, an amphetamine known as "tank-chocolates."

During training sessions and battle periods, the tank crews were given pills to help them cope with the physical demands of war. His need for the amphetamine and methamphetamine finally subsided around the same time as the swelling in his back.

Schmidt's mother visited but returned home after only a week in Berlin. Herman's father had died during the First World War and he was their only child. Schmidt enjoyed her visit but soon realized she missed her new life. She had remarried and had three other children. Without hesitation, Schmidt requested that she go home—he could recover without her assistance.

He was taken out of traction a week ago and made better progress in his recovery. Walking wasn't possible yet, but he was determined to recover and get back to fighting for the country.

"So, how far are you going to walk today?" asked Nurse Hilda Straus.

She sat in a chair next to him. Schmidt looked at her with his piercing brown eyes, not wanting to show any fear or weakness.

"How about we go farther than we did yesterday?" Schmidt said. The nurse smiled at the tall officer. As she helped him up from his reclined position, she noticed he was getting better looking. His hair was growing back and covering the scar on top of his head.

"How did you get this job of babysitting me during my recovery?"

Hilda smiled as she helped him to his feet.

"Well, you are not the shortest patient we have here, and since I am one of the taller nurses I drew the short straw. Besides, you're the great German tank commander hero from the Battle of Hannut. That may be the other reason I'm here," she answered.

Schmidt put his arm around the young nurse so she could help him walk and noticed for the first time that she was tall for a woman. Plus, she always smelled so good.

"Why are you calling me a hero?" asked Schmidt. She guided the captain to the medical parallel bars across the room. He placed his hands on the bars to balance himself, and she shifted her body and weight away while he pulled himself upright.

"I guess you haven't been reading the newspapers lately? The newspapers are calling you the Hero of Hannut. They say you broke through French defenses so our troops could get through and defeat them. That started the eventual move toward victory in France."

"Well, if that is the truth, I better get going and get out of your hair so I can continue my military career."

Hilda laughed. "Captain, if you walk anytime soon, it will be a miracle. The doctor already told you your tank career is in your past."

They stopped talking to concentrate on his therapy.

The doctor was busy with his rounds when he noticed two men in Gestapo leather outfits waiting at the nurses' station. When the Gestapo showed up, it usually wasn't good news for one of his patients. In fact, he'd had numerous patients dragged out of the hospital by the Gestapo before they recovered from their injuries. He never saw those patients again. He and the nurses were trained not to interfere with Gestapo during the course of their duties or they would face imprisonment. As the doctor approached the Gestapo, he noticed that these two were not the normal lower-ranking ones; both were high-ranking officers.

"What can I do for the Gestapo today?" asked the doctor.

The more senior officer replied, "Which room is Captain Schmidt located?" He carried a box and some paperwork.

"He is down the hall on the right, last room. Why do you want to see my patient?"

They ignored the doctor and walked to the room. The doctor waited until they entered the room before he moved toward the physical therapy room to warn Schmidt of his visitors.

Nurse Straus helped the captain into his wheelchair.

"Which way do you want to go back to your room for some much-deserved rest?" she asked. He turned to his left side, which was more comfortable than sitting.

"Let's go see some sunlight before I take my after-therapy nap."

Nurse Hilda smiled, knowing she did a great job with him today. *He is making excellent progress, which means he will be leaving soon,* thought Hilda.

As the doctor entered the therapy room he saw a nurse's white uniform disappear down the corridor toward the makeshift atrium that the hospital used for patient recovery. He glanced at the medical parallel bars, but there was no one there. There was only one other patient in the room and it wasn't Schmidt. *They must have gone the other way,* thought the doctor as he hurried back down the corridor. He saw Nurse Straus pushing Schmidt.

"Captain, may I have a word with you?"

The nurse swung the wheelchair around for the doctor. Just as the wheelchair turned, one of the Gestapo officers stuck his head out of Schmidt's room to see what was going on in the hallway.

"Captain Schmidt?" asked the officer. Nurse Straus, not knowing what to do, turned the wheelchair so her patient could see both of the men calling his name. It took Schmidt about a second to realize that the doctor had come to warn him.

"Doctor, let me see what this officer wants and I'll get back with you."

The doctor defiantly put his hands on his waist but submitted to his patient's request.

"Gentlemen, let's get this over with, or my nurse is going to pass out," Schmidt told the Gestapo officers. "Shall I stay in this wheelchair, or can I get into bed? My ass is killing me."

"Nurse, please help the captain into bed so he can be more comfortable," replied the senior officer. When she left the room the Gestapo officers wasted no time.

"Captain, how is your recovery?" asked the senior officer.

"Well, I'm making progress, but the doctor told me my tank career has come to a close. Shrapnel is wedged in my spine. What does the Gestapo have in store for me today?"

The senior officer grabbed a piece a paper from a folder and began to read. The other officer approached with a wooden box.

"For extreme gallantry and bravery in the face of overwhelming odds, Captain Herman Schmidt up-held the highest form of leadership by defeating our enemy. Your unit broke through their defenses with such force you destroyed five tanks, disabled countless other vehicles and killed over twenty enemy soldiers. Our infantry was able to advance with such force that our great infantry of German soldiers defeated the enemy in less time and with fewer causalities. You are hereby awarded the Knight's Cross of the Iron Cross.

Signed by Adolf Hitler."

The second officer placed the cross around Schmidt's neck, and all three gave the traditional German salute to their absent leader. When he saluted, Schmidt gasped in pain. The senior officer handed Schmidt the wooden box, then grabbed another piece of paper and read it.

"Captain Herman Schmidt, upon completion of your recovery from your wounds you will report to Gestapo officer training at the below location. Before you report to training you are hereby advanced to the rank of major."

Schmidt opened the wooden box and noticed a major's emblem enclosed next to the chest ribbon for his award.

"We will be sending someone to get measurements for your new uniforms. Welcome to the Gestapo, Herr Major."

The two Gestapo officers saluted him one more time and gathered all of their items before leaving the room.

The doctor and nurse were at the station when the door opened. To their surprise the Gestapo did not have Schmidt in tow. They passed the nurses' station without acknowledging the medical staff's presence. As soon as the Gestapo officers were out of sight, the two stepped into Schmidt's room. He was resting in bed with a ribbon and medal around his neck.

"Well, that doesn't happen very often," remarked the doctor.

The nurse removed the box and papers from Schmidt's chest so they wouldn't slide to the floor. She shut the blinds and turned out the lights before exiting the room.

Chapter 4

MAJOR SCHMIDT WAS IN his third month of recovery. He started walking without assistance from anyone or any apparatus weeks ago. He did physical therapy in the morning and again in afternoon after his post-lunch nap. The major and Nurse Straus spent a lot of time together in his room after his afternoon therapy sessions. They played cards, drank wine and shared stories about their lives. She found him to be distant and rigid at the beginning of their card games, but by the time they were on the second glass of wine his walls began to crumble. Still, Major Schmidt would indulge in long periods of silence, and this drove her crazy. She was never privy to where his thoughts took him.

The major had opened up about his fatherless childhood and disappointing upbringing. His only enjoyment was his military schooling. The military was where he excelled; it became his family. His mother had remarried and started another family, so he decided to join the German movement at the early age of sixteen. He quickly established himself as one the best tank drivers at the academy. While completing his engineering degree, military leaders tasked him with assisting in the development of the Panzer tank. When it came into production, he was one of the first test drivers, reporting all the flaws that needed to be corrected. He also noted all the advantages of this advanced tank.

Knowing the capabilities of the Panzer helped Schmidt become a brilliant field commander. He knew how and where to deploy the tanks. The battlefield was all he lived for, and despite his injuries he desperately wanted to return. In his long moments of silence, his mind drifted to his glory days destroying the enemy. His only consolation was the pretty nurse who tended to him.

He found out Nurse Straus was single and living in Berlin with another nurse. She was raised in a small farming community and left home years ago to find her way in the world. What better way for a girl to learn about the world than to come to the big city of Berlin? She finished her nursing education and was one of hundreds of female nurses taking care of the German soldiers wounded in battlefields all over Europe and Africa. She loved her work but wanted to have a family—eventually. With her busy schedule, she had no time to be involved with a man.

Nurse Straus was standing at the nurses' station catching up on paperwork when the doctor approached.

"How is our hero doing?" he asked with a little smirk.

The nurse blushed and remarked without looking in his direction, "He is doing excellent and walking without any assistance from me."

"How is his pain?"

"Well, it's hard to tell because he doesn't complain a lot, but he is not pain-free when he walks. He seems to be pain-free when sitting or lying down."

"The Gestapo called me this morning and they wanted to know when he will be ready for duty. What do you think, since you spend so much time with him?"

Nurse Straus had dreaded this day.

"I couldn't tell you until he is walking pain-free. It may take a couple of weeks to get there."

After her brief meeting with the doctor, she went to the major's room to see if he was ready for his morning physical therapy session. As she got closer to his room, she heard voices.

"Good morning, Nurse Straus. How are you doing?" asked the major.

The nurse could not help but blush a little—her patient was down to his undershorts and being fitted for his new uniforms as a Gestapo major. The room was full of hats, shirts, pants, gloves and jackets. A tailor was measuring his legs and waist. Beside the tailor, a young man who looked like his son held the tailor's pins.

"I guess this morning's session is on hold until you're done being fitted for your uniforms?" asked Hilda.

The tailor respectfully moved away from his work until he heard from the major to continue.

"Let's skip this morning session. Please come back at around one o'clock so we can get out of this hospital and grab some lunch. Will I have at least one uniform and a jacket, since it is getting cold outside, ready by one?"

The tailor nodded.

The major turned to Nurse Straus. "Can you leave the hospital and have lunch with me?"

At first, Straus thought he was talking to the tailor, but the handsome major was staring at her. She blushed and nodded submissively.

"Good, I am tired of this food and need a good, hot meal from a restaurant, and a cold beer."

Nurse Straus left his room with a smile. She thought, *I am going on a lunch date with a Gestapo major. What a great day.*

About an hour or so later she returned after the tailor and his son left laden with pinned fabrics.

"Are you ready to get out of this hospital?" Schmidt asked.

As the major turned to the door, she could tell he was still in pain when he walked. The cane was the only reason he could make his way toward her. *What a difference a uniform makes in his appearance,* thought Straus. When they exited, everyone stopped to look at the Gestapo officer dressed in all black and wearing the Iron Cross around his neck. Nurse Straus positioned herself on his left. She put her right arm under his left in a way that looked more natural than supportive.

"Thank you for coming with me. I needed to get out of the hospital. Shall we walk a little bit more before we find a place to eat?"

"Not too much farther. You don't want to hurt yourself."

As they continued down the sidewalk, everyone moved out of their way. This she had not seen before; she dismissed it as pedestrians feeling sorry for the recovering soldier.

"That looks like a good restaurant," said the major.

Straus guided him to the eatery across the busy intersection. All the motor vehicles stopped moving. Straus and Schmidt crossed the street with no delays, which again she dismissed as drivers feeling sorry for the wounded soldier. Upon entering the eatery, everyone stopped to look in their direction. Straus was connecting the dots when the owner appeared from a side door.

"Can we get a table near the sun?" the major asked the nervous owner.

"But of course, Herr Major. Let me clear a table for you and your guest. Will there be anybody else joining your party?"

The major didn't respond to his question but looked at the two guests being shooed away by a waiter. In a matter of seconds, the table was cleared and clean.

"This way, Herr Major," replied the owner. Hilda couldn't believe her eyes but guided her patient to his much-needed break and nourishment. After the major took his seat, Hilda went to hers, which was already being pulled out for her by the owner. After the menus were distributed, they were left alone.

"Does this happen to you all the time?" whispered the nurse. The major looked at his menu without responding. There wasn't much said until the waiter returned to take their orders.

"What can we get for you today, Herr Major?"

"We will have two orders of Wiener schnitzels and two beers."

The waiter wrote down the order and looked at Straus, who smiled and also requested a glass of water.

"Isn't this nice to be outside and enjoying the cool weather? We should do this more often as soon as I get back to full health."

Hilda smiled at Herman. She looked at the other patrons in the restaurant, who had not stopped staring at them. *I don't know if I can get used to all this attention.*

Chapter 5

GINO SAT IN THE Naples Hospital electrical utility room working on fuses and other electrical connections that needed maintenance. This was what the army did with soldiers physically unable to fight for their country. Gino didn't mind his new role, but there were times he wished he was back on the battlefields. Those thoughts quickly vanished when he remembered how miserable he was in battle; all he had to do was visit the wards at the hospital. He even visited other soldiers during his many smoke breaks, listening to their horrible war stories.

Most of the wounded had been injured in Southern France. This was Mussolini's attempt to capture the riches of France— the spoils of war. Gino also heard rumors that the Italians attacked British troops in Egypt, which shocked him. The Italian army was already spread thin. This warpath seemed like suicide.

Gino was a father and husband now, and if he wanted to see his daughter, Maria, who was recently born, he had to avoid the battlefield and the slaughter of Italian men.

The utility room door opened but Gino continued working without stopping to see who was entering his work space. Wounded soldiers routinely wandered the halls looking for any activity to pass the time while recovering. This time it was a couple of soldiers Gino had befriended. They watched him work on the fuses until he turned to see who was in his work environment. He smiled when he noticed his two friends, Carlo and Luigi holding wine, Gino's favorite beverage, plus bread and cheese—the main diet of most wounded Italian soldiers in Naples. It was about seven o'clock, which meant it was time to stop working and enjoy the evening.

Carlo's left arm was removed after he was wounded in battle, and Luigi had only one leg. Luigi didn't talk about how he lost his leg, and Gino never asked.

"I need to check out with the sergeant before we start drinking, guys. You know how he gets if he smells wine on our breath," said Gino.

"Not to worry. I already stopped by his office and he told us to tell you that you're off for the evening. That is, after I gave him a bottle of wine," responded Luigi.

They all laughed because they knew the sergeant loved his wine.

In the back of the utility room was their makeshift meeting place—a table with some chairs Gino had acquired at the hospital. Carlo and Luigi put this evening's offerings on the table and took their usual places. They shared a lot of time in this room, talking about politics, war, and families, and playing cards—occasionally gambling but never setting the limits too high. As Gino approached the table with the wine glasses, he asked if they'd heard any news about the ongoing war.

"You know what, Gino, it's hard to get the truth from some of the soldiers since they don't know what's going on, but nothing new today," replied Carlo.

"What about you, Luigi. Anything new today?"

"Nothing you don't already know, but I did overhear some of the doctors talking about getting some wounded from Egypt in the next few days."

Gino poured wine for everyone and Luigi sliced the bread with his military knife. Gino watched Luigi and thought the rumors must be true about Italians attacking the British in Egypt. *Italy is deep into this war and I need to get out of here real soon, or they will send me back to war with one lung,* thought Gino.

"Any news on when you two are getting out of here and going back home?" asked Gino.

"I asked the sergeant when I dropped the wine off to him, and according to him there's still a hold on sending folks back home. Which means I get to hang out with you guys longer, so let's play cards and drink some wine," Luigi said.

They all laughed as Gino took a deck of cards from the drawer and shuffled. They were playing *La Scopa*, and only two could play at a time. Usually the third drank, ate and kept score so there was no cheating.

"What about the rumors of the resistance movement?" asked Gino.

Nothing was said for about a minute because they all knew it was certain death if they were caught even whispering about such issues.

"All I hear is rumors, but nothing I would write home about. Now deal the cards," said Luigi.

***

The next day Gino was working on the same fuse when he heard someone come into the utility room. He turned to see his sergeant behind him, drinking a cup of coffee.

"What are you doing, Private Cartelli?" asked the sergeant.

"I'm fixing the spare fuses so we have some extras in case we need them. What can I do for you today, Sergeant?" replied Gino.

"It looks like the Axis powers are making Rome their main headquarters and they're looking to move some of our folks there to support our troops. I was thinking about asking for volunteers, but I remembered your family is from the north and I was wondering if you want to go there and help out. You're a pretty good electrician, and they have requested electricians if we have them."

Gino was relieved that the sergeant wasn't here about his talking about the resistance, a military crime punishable by firing squad.

"When can I leave?" asked Gino.

The sergeant smiled and told him that he would get back to Gino when the orders came.

***

It had been months since the sergeant mentioned going to the Rome. Gino had seen most of his comrades come and go while he was in Naples; they were either sent back to war or, like him, being used for work in another city or country. Carlo was the only one left, and he worked in the administration office across the street. Gino had even heard discussions about sending Italian troops to work in Germany as laborers. All he wanted was to get back home to his wife and daughter in Cimpello.

Gino went to work every morning, caused no problems and always told his sergeant what was going on with the usual bottle of wine. The hospital's electrical work was never-ending and usually required him to repair old equipment with even older parts since most of the Italian factories were more focused on war than electrical production. The days ran together, which made for a lot of time to figure out how to get home.

It was impossible to get to Cimpello from Naples without being gone for a long time. The trains were unreliable; trucks and cars were owned by the army and forget about making the trip by bus. Now, in Rome, the trains ran north through just about every city, including Pordenone and Venice, which were close to Cimpello. Getting assigned to Rome was his ticket to getting home while still in the army.

Gino took matters into his own hands after learning most of the military workers were being shipped out from Carlo's administrative office, which handled transfer orders. Gino decided he needed to talk with Carlo to help him forge orders to Rome.

It was card night, and around seven the door to the storage room opened. In came Carlo holding the usual bottle of wine and some food. Gino smiled and congratulated him on his ability to carry so much.

"If you think this is great, you should see me type," remarked Carlo.

"They don't let you type. You only have one arm."

Carlo laughed and placed all the goods on the table. "Well, I type some stuff—mostly one-page memos and correspondence from one officer to another. But I'm hoping to move up in the administration world and start licking envelopes."

The friends laughed and fell into their usual routine. When Luigi was shipped home, Carlo and Gino decided not to invite anybody else for fear of spies. There were a lot of untrustworthy individuals running around the hospital, so why take chances?

As Gino dealt the cards he said, "Carlo, I need a favor from you."

"Sure, what do you need?"

Gino took a deep breath. "Well, remember when the sergeant said I could be going to Rome?"

"Yes, I remember when he told you, but that was months ago, and you haven't mentioned it at all, so I figured you were happy here."

"Well, if I were going to Rome, it would have already happened. I was wondering if you see orders coming through your office and how often are there orders to Rome?"

Carlo stopped looking at his cards and turned his attention to his friend. "Gino, I see all kinds of orders come through the office on a daily basis. We get and give orders for just about every city in Italy, including Rome. And I even see orders for other countries as well. Why do you ask?" Carlo knew what was coming.

"Carlo, do you type the orders, or do other people type the orders?"

Carlo put the cards down and raised his glass of wine. After he took a long sip he said, "Ask what you want from me, Gino."

"Can you type orders for me to go to Rome?"

Carlo smiled and picked up his cards. "I wondered when you were going to ask me to get you out of here. How do you think Luigi left all of the sudden?"

Gino was so shocked by Carlo's remark that they both chuckled.

"Come by my office tomorrow and we'll check what's on the board of empty billets that need to be filled. Rome headquarters has been requesting a lot of personnel lately due to the buildup of German soldiers."

The next day during Gino's daily trip to his sergeant's office for his morning brief, he continued to the administrative department across the street. If he was asked why he was in the building, he would reply that he was checking for mail. Gino had been in the building before to shoot the breeze with Carlo every now and again. The main office had a huge lobby with wooden chairs facing all the clerks working at their desks. Most of the workers were women, but there were a few army wounded, including Carlo. He had finished college, which was why he landed the office job.

Gino saw Carlo in the back of the room working at his desk. Usually when Gino walked to Carlo's desk he didn't pay attention to his surroundings, but today he noticed everything. He saw who had typewriters, where the bulletin boards were located, what type of documents were on the desks, and who was doing orders. As he approached Carlo's desk, he saw a ring binder next to Carlo's typewriter with the words *Top Priority Filled Billets*.

Carlo grabbed the cigarette from his mouth to put it out as he looked at Gino.

"Well, my friend, what brings you here today?" Carlo said, winking.

Gino remarked, "Checking the mail and seeing if there's anything else that needs to go to the sergeant at the hospital."

"Let me finish this letter and I'll walk you over to the mailroom."

Gino grabbed the seat next to Carlo's desk, and Carlo pointed at the ring binder and went back to work on his typewriter. Carlo was good at typing with one hand—as fast as the two-handed personnel. Gino turned his attention to the binder and saw a whole page of requested billets for Rome's headquarters. They needed administration support, construction laborers, maids, cooks, telephone operators and, of course, electricians. Carlo typed and smiled from ear to ear. When he finished, he grabbed the paper out of the typewriter and lit a cigarette as quickly as any person with two arms. Gino was impressed with his friend's dexterity and followed him as Carlo carried the ring binder and paper he grabbed from the typewriter to one of the bulletin boards. Carlo hung the binder and headed for the mailroom like he had done a hundred times before.

Carlo put the paper in the out-basket on somebody's desk as they left the big office space. They walked into the hallway and Carlo stopped to finish his cigarette.

"Which billet do you want?"

Gino looked around before he answered his friend. "The electrician billet will work for me."

Carlo smiled. "Well, I was hoping that's what you wanted because I finished your request and just put it on the order clerk's desk. Let's hope she doesn't check for signatures, but they usually don't because they're doing so many requests every day."

All Gino could do was glance at the desk and back at his friend. They smiled and continued toward the mailroom.

"It will take a day or two, but you should hear something from your sergeant soon," Carlo said.

Two days later, Gino was trying to figure out why one of the hospital sections had lost power. Everything looked good inside, but with all the thieves in the city it wasn't uncommon for them risk their lives stealing electrical wiring that had power. Sure enough, the wire had been cut from its routing point and taken. Luckily, Gino had rolls of it locked in the storage room. He needed to secure power to this section of the hospital before replacing the wire. In the breaker room, he pulled the fuse and headed to the storage room to retrieve the replacement wire. As he exited, he was met by his sergeant, who was standing at the doorway with a paper in his hand.

He looked disturbed. "Private Cartelli, what are you doing?"

"I'm fixing the power outage on the north-side second floor of the hospital. Someone cut and took that section of wire again. The power will be back in a couple of hours once I replace the wire," answered Gino.

The sergeant seemed to calm down, but something was clearly bothering him. Gino didn't say anything.

"Well, when you get done with the repairs come to my office. Your orders are in for Rome."

As the sergeant walked away, Gino heard him mumbling about getting someone trained just before they leave and why he hated the army. Gino waited until the sergeant was out of view before running to the storage room. He wanted to finish the repairs as quickly as possible in case something changed or the sergeant asked questions about his orders.

Gino finished the repairs and was at the sergeant's office

in about an hour. He was about to knock on his door when he heard the sergeant on the phone asking questions about orders. Gino couldn't make out what he was asking, but he didn't want to take a chance, so he went to the switchboard to seemingly fix an electrical issue. The phones went dead after Gino fixed the problem.

He was back at the sergeant's office in five minutes. He knocked and the sergeant told him to come in.

"Damn phones never work around here," the sergeant groused. "Private Cartelli, here are your orders to Rome. You leave tomorrow. Take this to the administration building tomorrow morning, and they will get you train tickets and some travel money. Good luck in Rome."

Gino took the orders and thanked the sergeant for his help during his stay in Naples. As he left the office, the sergeant said, "See if you can figure out what's wrong with my telephone line."

"No problem, Sergeant. I'll get right on it."

As Gino left the building, he dropped the telephone switch he'd removed and headed to his room to pack for Rome.

The next morning, Gino went to the administration building with his one bag of personal belongings. He wasn't the only soldier looking for train tickets. He lined up at the travel office. When he finally made it to the front, the travel clerk had his ticket and money ready for him. Before he left, he went to say goodbye to Carlo, but Carlo wasn't at his desk. Gino didn't want to raise suspicions, so he left the building and looked for the bus that transported the troops to the train station. The troops were already being loaded. When he stepped onto the bus, he noticed Carlo sitting in the back, smiling. Gino sat next to him but said nothing.

Carlo leaned over to whisper, "You think I'm going to stay here after you leave? I don't think so; I'm headed to Sardinia and some new adventures."

Gino smiled as the bus door closed.

Chapter 6

ITALY INVADED GREECE THROUGH Albania in the fall of 1940 in an attempt to conquer the Balkans. Although they gained ground, they were eventually halted by the Greek forces and retreated back to Albania. The Greek victory over the initial Italian offensive was the first Allied land victory of World War II and helped raise morale in occupied Europe. Over 500,000 Italian troops where held up in Albania, and many Italians began questioning their leaders and the direction of the war. The Italians suffered 10,000 dead and 60,000 wounded in the failed attempt. Most of the wounded were shipped to military hospitals all over Italy. The Germans were concerned and prepared to oversee their neighbors to the south to ensure this would not happen again.

**

Gino sat in the back of the train as it barreled down the tracks toward his new duty station in Rome. He didn't know what to expect but decided to take a chance on not reporting for duty until he had seen his wife.

There were only a few soldiers on board, unlike other trips when the entire train or bus was full of soldiers. He had to be careful and travel at night; his plan was to lose the uniform and get regular clothes in Rome. He would get on a train and head home to be with Catherina for the weekend. He would also check on his father and mother, who he had not heard from in some time.

As the train pulled into Rome, he noticed the station was full of soldiers—German soldiers. The stories he had heard in Naples were true; the Nazis had made Rome their headquarters. As the train rolled to a stop, he moved quickly, heading to the nearest exit. There were so many people in the station house that no one seemed to notice him. He avoided the army check-in centers past the exits, heading instead for a shopping district. While in Naples, he had saved some money for such an occasion. Everything was so expensive in Rome that he only had enough money to buy one set of clothes.

He headed to the nearest men's store and was looking at shirts when the owner walked toward him.

"You need to leave my store right now before I call the authorities on you," the man said.

Gino looked at the owner. "What am I doing wrong, sir?"

The owner grabbed Gino by the upper arm and pulled him to the entrance. Gino held his ground and looked at the owner, puzzled.

"What is wrong with you?"

"Do you want to get both of us killed, Private? You know you are not allowed into any clothing stores. The Germans forbid it."

"What are you talking about?" The store owner stopped pulling on Gino and noticed his uniform looked different from the ones he was used to seeing out in the streets. "You're not stationed here, are you?"

Gino looked at him and around the store and replied, "No, I just came from Naples and I'm reporting for duty. What I need is some clothes so I can go home for a couple of days and not be worried about someone thinking I'm a deserter. All I want is to see my wife and check on my father and mother."

The owner, who had been in the Italian Royal Army during World War I, felt sorry for Gino.

"Private, you need to leave now before the authorities come here. What you need to do is come back after it gets dark, but come to the back door of the store. Do you understand me?"

Gino nodded and exited. It was already getting late, so he proceeded downtown to get lost in the evening crowds.

At about eight o'clock, he worked his way back to the clothing store. Gino walked to the back of the store as instructed but had a hard time finding the right door. There were five doors in a row to pick from. He knocked on the one with dim light coming from the bottom. The owner answered and looked outside to see if anybody was watching. As soon as he thought everything was clear, he grabbed Gino by the arm, pulling him into the back of the store. The owner waited two minutes and stepped onto a chair, looking out the window above the door to make sure no one was hiding in the alley. Gino's heart pounded.

"Do you think you were followed?" asked the owner.

"No, sir."

In the tailor's workroom, Gino saw a tie and shirt hanging in the corner. A pair of nice shoes, socks, and a hat sat next to a light-brown suit with pinstripes that perfectly matched the tie and hat.

"You need to look like you're doing something and not passing through in civilian clothes. The Fascists or Nazis will stop you and ask if you're in the army, and if you are in civilian clothes, it won't be good for you. If you tell them you're a shoe salesman, you have a chance of getting home and back. Now, try on everything and see if we have to make any changes to the suit."

Gino smiled at the ploy, got undressed, and grabbed the suit from the sitting bench. While Gino dressed, the owner went up front and returned with a suitcase.

"Oh, you look good in that suit; you are the same size as my son. I made that suit for him some time ago and it needs a good home," the owner said.

Gino smiled and didn't pry into where the owner's son was because there were so many young men missing.

"You will need a salesman suitcase like this one. It opens from the top to reveal two pairs of shoes. When you remove the shoes, it can hold another two pairs in the below compartment, but what most people don't know is it has another compartment on the bottom where you can store extra clothes, like an army uniform." The owner winked.

"I don't have enough money for the suit, shoes and suitcase."

The owner grinned slightly as Gino put on the suit jacket to make sure it fit properly.

"I tell you what; pay me what you can afford now and come by my store in this suit every so often to tell me how things are going in your life," replied the owner. His eyes filled with tears. He reached into a cabinet and pulled out a bottle of wine and two glasses. "Do we have an agreement?"

"Of course, we have an agreement."

"Good. Let's drink to your new suit before you get out of here and go visit your family."

Gino smiled and handed the owner most of his money, keeping a small amount for travel. They sat and talked for about an hour. The shop owner finally told Gino that his son was killed in Ethiopia and his wife had passed away some time ago from an illness. His only living relative was a daughter who worked for the government and visited infrequently.

Gino left the store from the back entrance and again promised the owner he would come by with the suit on to see how he was doing and maybe have a glass of wine with him.

***

As he headed for the train station, Gino picked up his pace. He wanted to leave that night. The train station wasn't as busy as it had been earlier. He stepped to the ticket counter to purchase a ticket to Venice, hoping to avoid suspicion at his true destination of Pordenone. He would exit the train in Pordenone, a stop on the way to Venice, and then make his way to Catherina's farm by foot.

The path from Pordenone to her farm was through the woods. He had often traveled the secluded path with Catherina's brother, Chester, to avoid the glare of nosy neighbors.

Getting closer to the ticket booth, he saw Fascist watchdogs right next to the counter, watching everyone buying tickets. Gino stood like any other waiting passenger.

As he approached the ticket booth window, an employee asked his destination.

"Venice, please."

"What takes you to Venice?"

"Well, I have the latest shoes we make here, and I'll be showing them to some of our favorite shoe stores so they can put in their orders."

He opened his suitcase to show the two pairs in the top. The employee looked at them, gave him an approving smile, and handed him his ticket to Venice. The train was on track five and would be leaving in ten minutes. Gino thanked the employee and headed to the track. This train station was the largest he had ever been in; it had ten sets of tracks and a second floor of shops and bars with lots of people standing around chatting, drinking, and eyeing passersby.

He boarded the train and found a seat next to a window. He saw uniformed soldiers on the tracks; some had dogs. As the train surged in the direction of his beloved Catherina, Gino's eyelids felt heavy, and before he knew it, he was sleeping this long day away.

Gino awoke as the train approached Pordenone. He wanted to get off without raising suspicion, and he wanted to avoid running into folks that knew him. When the train stopped in the previous cities, he noticed some stations had watchdogs and some didn't. To avoid them, he moved to the back of the train car; he could exit and head for the woods if he noticed anything suspicious. His secret trail to Catherina's farm was near the station.

As the train approached the station, Gino noticed the wooded area was still there, but there was a small fence around it— nothing he couldn't get over if he needed to. The train stopped, and he made his way to the exit with his hat pulled low and feet moving fast.

Few passengers left the train station; it was late and already dark. As he crossed the street out front, he glanced at the lights of downtown Pordenone. This was the most popular route for passengers leaving the train station. He looked at the farm fields and wooded area; no one walked in that direction. Gino slipped unnoticed into the park and was swallowed by the darkness. After a couple of minutes, he stopped, looked back, and decided he hadn't been followed. He quickly crossed the fields for the long walk to Cimpello and his beloved Catherina.

His legs were full of energy and excitement from this new

journey. Gino had traveled so much in the last year and seen a lot in his short lifetime, but at that moment it was a blur. He focused on the trail and thoughts of his family.

Nothing seemed to have changed. The path was the same size and the trees where the same trees, except they had grown. He picked an area about a hundred meters into the woods, near a clearing, to bury the suitcase under leaves and branches. He waited for about five minutes to make sure no one was watching him and continued his journey.

He exited the woods with the town of Cimpello on his right and the Zucchet farm on the left. It was getting late; Gino had lost track of time but knew he had been walking for about two hours, and he saw a light from the Zucchet farm. He planned to see Catherina first, and if he had time and safe passage, he would visit his father and mother.

He made his way towards the farm using the ditches that the farmers dug to channel the water coming down from the mountains when the ice melted. The farmers used the water for their crops and animals, but the ditches also made great hiding places for travelers.

Chapter 7

AS GINO APPROACHED THE farm, he could see the light in the kitchen. He didn't want to scare anybody, so he headed to Bruno's room. Bruno was Catherina's younger brother and still lived and worked on the farm. Catherina mentioned in one of her letters that he was living in the back of the farmhouse to make more room for her and Maria. As he made his way to the door, he stopped just before he knocked to hear if anybody was up or if there was any movement from inside the room. Gino knew this place like the back of his hand from all the time he spent there with Chester. Gino took a deep breath and knocked ever so gently.

"Bruno, this is Gino. Are you here?" whispered Gino.

Gino heard what sounded like someone getting out of bed and putting on their shoes.

"Gino?" Bruno said.

"Yes, it's me," answered Gino.

"Oh my god, hold on. Give me a minute."

Bruno opened the door and shined a gas lantern in Gino's direction.

"Oh my god, it is you!" He immediately gave him a hug and they both laughed.

"It's good to see you again, Bruno. Are Catherina and Maria in the main house?"

"Oh, yes, and it looks like she's trying to feed Maria again. She doesn't like to sleep too much, so your wife has to stay up late. Let's go see them."

Catherina stood at the kitchen sink finishing the dishes she used to feed Maria. Maria was in the wooden high chair her grandfather built, watching her mother at the sink. Catherina heard the kitchen door open and continued to clean the dishes.

"Bruno, is that you?"

"Yes, it's me, and I couldn't sleep. I saw the light on."

Gino followed Bruno into the kitchen glancing in the direction of his daughter to the left of the kitchen. He was overjoyed with what he saw and went immediately to Catherina. Catherina was just about finished when she turned to see what her brother was doing. She gasped at the sight of her husband and instantly started to cry with joy as she wrapped her arms around him.

Catherina's parents, Pietro and Anna, and Bruno were all at the table when Catherina told Gino that his father had been killed in the town square by the Germans. Gino was so upset that he couldn't even talk. He realized at that moment that he hated the Germans and wanted out of the army. The anger in him was very strong and deep and would last for the rest of his life. There was no good reason to keep playing Mussolini's game. Gino was going to find a way to leave the army and avenge the deaths of his father and brothers.

Catherina made Gino promise not to desert; Fascist supporters would come to the farm and look for him. There were rumors that deserter families were the first to suffer. After Gino explained how he arrived at the farm, Pietro smiled as he would at his own sons.

"What needs to happen tomorrow is that Bruno will go with you to the train station in Pordenone. He will make sure that you get back on the train to Rome without anybody seeing you. The last thing we need is to have someone recognize you. In the future, you need to let us know when you are coming, and we can prepare for your arrival."

Gino agreed to let them know ahead of time when he was coming to visit, but he wouldn't know until he figured out what he was doing in Rome.

"It's time we all go to bed so Gino and Catherina can spend some time by themselves," remarked Pietro.

Anna kissed them both and followed her husband. Bruno excused himself to his room. Catherina picked up Maria and led Gino to the bedroom that would be their sanctuary for the brief future.

Chapter 8

THE RETURN TRAIN NEARED Rome and Gino kept watch for any sign of trouble. A sea of emotions vexed his body. On the one hand, he was happy to have spent the night with Catherina and Maria, but he was also sad about his father, who had been assaulted by a German officer in the middle of town and died days later from his head wounds. Gino didn't have time to see what had happened to his father's farm or discover his mother's location. The farm was probably being run by Fascist supporters to produce crops for the German and Italian armies. Catherina and Anna would check on his mother in the near future to make sure she was alive.

All the men in his family were dead; Gino was the lone survivor. The rest of his family had scattered, and finding them could take months. That would have to wait until after the war.

The ride back to Rome went without incident, and, just as he had promised, Gino visited the clothes shop owner. Making his way through the morning crowds, he saw the store, but something didn't feel right. He kept going. Gino glanced into the window but quickly looked away when he saw two Fascist soldiers talking to the owner, who was seated. There might have been more soldiers in the store, but Gino wasn't waiting to find

out. It was time to go to the military check-in center. He needed
to find a place to change into his uniform without being noticed.
It was Sunday, so a church, perhaps. He found one with a large
crowd waiting for the next services. There were soldiers in the
crowd as well, he made his way to the front of the mass so he
could be first and find a room for a quick change.

Gino left the church in his uniform. The suit was neatly
stored in the secret bottom compartment of his suitcase. As
he neared the center of the city, he stopped another soldier
and asked where the check-in building was located. He got his
bearings, thanked the soldier, and off he went to check into his
new duty station. After about thirty minutes, he came to a line
of soldiers that stretched so far he couldn't see the beginning.

He approached the last soldier in line.

"Excuse me, but what is this line for?" asked Gino.

The soldier turned around and replied, "This is the check-
in for Rome duty, but they are checking everyone carefully
and sending some of the soldiers back to battlefronts if they're
capable of further duty. Got a smoke?"

Gino felt uneasy and handed the soldier a cigarette.

"What's your name?" the soldier asked as the flame of the
match hit the cigarette.

"Gino Cartelli. You are extremely tall. Are you sure you're
Italian?" Gino asked.

The other soldier smiled. Gino was six feet tall and was always
asked the same because of his height. He couldn't imagine how
this guy, at least six inches taller than he, went through life. Not
only was he really tall, but he was also at least 250 pounds of
pure muscle.

"I should ask you the same question, my friend, and thanks
for the cigarette," the soldier replied.

Gino relaxed a little, knowing he'd befriended possibly the
largest man he'd ever met.

"What are your injuries? You don't look wounded at all," the
soldier said.

"I lost a lung and had a nasty bout of malaria. What's your
name?"

"Giacomo Romano."

Giacomo was missing an eye and had a hard time standing

straight, which meant he was likely dealing with back issues from the war. The line moved toward some dead-end street, but it was still a long way off.

"Where did you get wounded, Giacomo?"

"Greece. What a fiasco. We got creamed. What's been your job? I'm just an infantry soldier, which means since I can still walk they're going to send me back to die in some far-off war."

Gino looked at his own paperwork—*electrician* and *telephone repair skill* was typed in several places on the second page, and Carlo had given Gino two copies of his orders just in case.

"Let me see your orders."

Giacomo's expression changed as he handed them to his new friend. Giacomo was listed as *in infantry* in the special skills section, which wasn't good. Gino looked around before he ripped Giacomo's skill section out and replaced it with the extra copy listing him as an electrician and telephone technician.

"Now you're an electrician and telephone service technician."

Giacomo was stunned at first, but he grabbed his paperwork. "Where do you call home, fellow electrician?"

"I live up north near a town called Cimpello. What about you?"

Giacomo finished his cigarette before he answered with a huge smile. "My family is from Vicenza."

This was good because this meant they had a lot in common. Both of them were from the north, which was far different from the south. As they moved closer to the check-in desk, Gino saw two Italian soldiers sitting and checking in soldiers. Standing behind them were three German soldiers deciding what to do with the soldiers checking in for duty. Some of the soldiers were told to go to the left and into a building; others were told to go to the right. Gino tried to hear what was being said, and so did the other soldiers in line, but most of the conversation was in German. Giacomo was ordered to the left desk while Gino was ordered to the right.

As Gino approached, he saw a doctor and some nurses in the back checking on soldiers. They were Italian and German medical personnel, but Germans were making most of the decisions. This was not good; folks a lot worse than he was were sent back to the front. As Gino made it to the desk, he was asked for his papers.

He handed his papers to the clerk.

"What did you do in Naples, Private Cartelli?" asked the clerk.

Before Gino could reply, a German officer dressed in a black leather jacket leaned over to look at his documents and hear the conversation. The man wore a cross around his neck. Gino snapped to attention as best as he could. *Gestapo.*

***

Major Schmidt was getting bored with the daily assessment of these obviously broken-down and unqualified Italian soldiers. He was sent to Rome to establish a possible German command and to help smooth over things with the Italian royal family. One of his other duties was to make sure the Italians built their army back to full strength. The Germans were going to make a run for Greece later in the year and needed Italian's forces. Schmidt was disgusted by these half-hearted warriors and understood why they lost to the Greeks. The whole Italian country was a disorganized mess that needed German oversight if Italy was to be a factor in conquering all of Europe.

As he leaned in to look at Gino's qualifications, he heard something from his right which took his attention away from his duties. Two Italian soldiers ran from the check-in station. A junior German officer next to Schmidt followed the deserters with a couple of Italian soldiers in tow.

The major walked toward the commotion but decided to conserve his energy. He was finally feeling better from his wounds but still walked with a slight limp. The headaches were not happening as often, but when he had a long day or became tired, they always came back to remind him of Hannut. Today was such a day.

Gino took a deep breath. "I worked on the electrical power, switchboards and telephone systems at the hospital."

The clerk spoke to the German officer and then said, "What is your medical condition, Private Cartelli?"

"I had one of my lungs removed, and malaria damaged the other lung. I can't march for long without resting or catching my breath."

The clerk translated, but the German major was distracted by another commotion—a few more fleeing Italian soldiers being chased. The clerk waited for the officer to make a decision. Gino stood, nervously watching two uniformed guards capture the fleeing Italians and escort them back to face their punishment. The clerk asked the major again which direction to send Gino, and the German officer, disgusted by what he had just witnessed, motioned toward the medical area.

The clerk told Gino to see the doctor. As he was proceeding, gunshots came from the building where the German guards had escorted the two soldiers. Everyone glanced toward the gunshots for a split second and knew what had happened.

As Gino entered the medical area, a nurse approached him and asked, "Let me see your papers. Please have a seat and take off your shirt so the doctor can examine you."

Gino looked around and noticed everyone complying with anything requested of them. He sat with his clothes in his lap until the doctor approached him.

The first thing the doctor noticed was Gino's massive scar. The Italian translator with the doctor looked tired when he asked Gino to repeat what happened to him. The translator explained Gino's wounds to the doctor, who listened to him breathe with a stethoscope. He moved to Gino's back and made some comments to the translator.

"The doctor wants to know how far you can walk or run before you have difficulty breathing," the translator said.

"About four hundred meters before I have to stop and catch my breath because of the pain in my chest."

The doctor asked Gino to stand while the exam continued.

Back at the check-in line, Major Schmidt asked the junior officer about the two Italians who had just been shot for trying to escape.

"What kind of soldiers were those two?"

"They were infantry, but there was nothing wrong with them. They were deserters that got into the wrong line thinking they would be given the Rome duty."

"I wish they would send us skilled people so we can rebuild this pathetic city," Schmidt said. He remembered the man he had just sent to have medically evaluated. "Get that last soldier

I sent to the medical tent and check if he's an electrician. If he is, send him to the other line for duty here in the city." He grabbed his head to massage away the pounding in his cranium.

The doctor grabbed Gino's records and was writing something down when a junior German officer with the same black leather jacket as the major entered the exam room. He grabbed the paperwork and spoke with the doctor. Gino wondered what just happened as he dressed. The nurse came into the exam area with a slight smile. She held his records.

"You are one lucky guy. The doctor was going to send you to the front, but that officer told him you were needed here in Rome."

Gino almost jumped with excitement but refrained for fear of being shot.

"What kind of special skills do you have, Private Cartelli?"

"I'm an electrician, and I can repair and service telephone lines."

"Well, that's why you're staying. This city is always having problems with the telephones and electricity. I need you to finish getting dressed and come with me so you can check into your new duty station."

Gino finished dressing in the uniform he hated and followed the nurse with his suitcase in tow.

The nurse led Gino to the other side of the check-in area. As he passed the desk, the other soldiers looked his way with fear in their eyes. He walked so fast he almost ran into the nurse. She went past the door where the now-dead deserters had been taken and continued walking. They stopped at the next room.

The nurse turned to Gino and said, "Take a seat. They will call you when they're ready for you."

Gino saw Giacomo at the end of a bench and walked over. Giacomo smiled from ear to ear.

"I thought they were going to send you to the front," he remarked.

"I thought the same thing, and I was a little nervous," replied Gino, handing his new friend another cigarette.

"I am glad you're here, because I don't know the first thing about electricity."

Gino laughed as he lit two cigarettes. For the first time since he arrived in Rome, he felt calm in this country whose future was so uncertain.

Chapter 9

MAJOR SCHMIDT WAS STILL in Rome. His original assignment was to ensure the Italian army was rebuilding after their embarrassment in the Balkans, but now his orders had permanently attached him to the city. Not only was he in charge of making sure the Italian army kept their numbers up, but he was also instructed to train their tank commanders on battlefield strategy. Additionally, Rome was instructed to gather the Gypsies and Jews for deportation. He needed a holding area for them before sending them to Germany. Once they arrived in Germany, he wasn't sure what would happen to them, and he didn't care.

Major Schmidt was enjoying one of his few days without severe headaches or backaches. His office was only about half a kilometer from his place of residence, and if the weather wasn't too bad, he walked to work. He gauged his pain on the walk. *The day is starting out pleasant, but for how long?*

After entering his office, which used to be the house of a local public official who spoke out against the war, he could tell that there weren't yet any emergencies or people who needed his immediate attention. His secretary, Marta Columbo, awaited him in the lobby. She always stood when he entered the room to show respect for his rank.

"Good morning, Herr Major. How was your walk this morning?" asked Marta, who was fluent in Italian, French and German, not to mention good at typing in all three languages.

The major cast Marta his signature morning glance and moved toward the jacket hooks. He hung his black leather jacket and combination hat before he responded.

"The walk was good, and the cold wasn't bad this morning. Do I have any mail or messages?"

Marta handed him his mail and his messages on the familiar German Nazi emblem paper on which she wrote down his calls.

"You have a letter from Hilda, a local call from the compound area, and one call from Berlin, but I couldn't get all the information before we lost contact. It was from Gestapo headquarters—a Colonel Weber."

This news made the major smile a little; the unreliable phone system was a perfect excuse if he wasn't in the mood to talk with Berlin. The weather played a major factor in how the phones worked. The letter also made him smile. It was nice to have someone in his life as sweet as Hilda, the woman who nursed him back to health.

"The colonel needs to talk to you about Greece and the way station."

The way station was being built to remove the local Gypsies and Jews. It was close to the Tiber River, next to an old train station stop they would use to load them. The ghetto was a cramped, four-block section of the city that was being fenced in to control movement.

Major Schmidt's head started to pound knowing he had to call his ever-involved supervisor to provide more updates and, of course, receive more guidance. The major read the message from the officer in charge of the way station and noted that it would be ready for the first train arrival that evening.

"Please call my driver to come get me in thirty minutes. I want to see how the progress is going on the way station," the major ordered as he went to his office to read his letter from Hilda.

***

On top of an alleyway wall, Giacomo inspected an electrical box with a maze of wiring he couldn't interpret. His one good eye was focused on the puzzle when Gino came from behind.

"You have no idea what you're looking at, do you?" asked Gino.

"No, but I have learned not to stick my hands into an electrical box since the last time we did this. My hair still stands up every time someone turns on a light in a room."

Gino snickered and looked at the main breaker. The new electrical power ran to an area designated as some type of holding area. This morning they had been assigned to run power to this zone. Like good soldiers, they didn't ask questions as to why they needed power in the ghetto. Giacomo followed Gino to the main road through the narrow alley where the supervisors wanted lights.

"We're going to need more poles to hoist these electrical wires and attach the light fixtures," Gino said to his ever-present giant of a friend.

Giacomo looked around to see which side would be best for the poles. He looked down the alley from the main road and saw soldiers near the end setting up tables and chairs. A couple of Gestapo officers directed the area setup.

"Gino, come here and see what's going on down at the other end of the alley."

"Okay, what's so important?"

"Look," replied Giacomo as he pointed.

Gino saw the Gestapo officers directing soldiers to set up barriers. "What's so important? It's not like we haven't seen this before. Remember, they had something like this when we checked into our duty here."

"Not that. Look up in the buildings on the top of this alleyway."

In plain sight, soldiers escorted local folks out of their slum dwellings. Most were carrying just about everything they owned and heading toward the main street. Gino looked down the main road and saw them emerging.

"Why are they evicting these folks from their homes?" asked Giacomo.

"I have no idea, but it looks like they're doing it throughout this neighborhood." Gino pointed at more unfortunate individuals being escorted out to the main street.

The Germans were also erecting road barriers to ensure no one went into certain areas in the ghetto as they made their way toward the railroad station and were loaded on trains. It looked like the Germans were herding cattle for the market.

As Giacomo headed for the area where the electric poles were dropped off earlier in the day, there was a shout in their direction.

"You two come here!" yelled a German officer in the familiar black jacket of the Gestapo. Gino and Giacomo looked at each other and proceeded toward the officer in the alley.

"Yes, Herr Officer. What can we do for you?" asked Gino.

Giacomo stood next to Gino, looking down at the significantly shorter German officer.

"What are you two doing here?" he asked, looking at Giacomo and noting the patch covering one of his eye sockets.

"We're the electricians running the lighting for this area," said Gino. He had learned in the past not to let Giacomo talk— Giacomo had a way of insulting the officers when he spoke, and the two electricians didn't need additional attention; the officer was now in a staring contest with Giacomo, which wasn't a good thing.

"Herr Officer, can I talk to you!" yelled a junior German soldier.

"Continue with your work and report to me when you are completed," replied the officer without taking his eyes off the one-eyed soldier.

"Yes sir," answered Gino as he grabbed Giacomo and directed him away from this tense situation. Gino looked back to see the German still staring. "What is wrong with you?" he asked Giacomo.

"I don't work for the Germans; I hate them."

Gino smiled and nodded in agreement but admonished, "Let's do our jobs and stay out of trouble."

The men moved the poles in place and began attaching electrical lines. Each pole was about three meters in length and needed two strong individuals to carry them. The alley was about a hundred meters long. As they finished laying out the poles, Gino heard noise at the entrance of the alleyway. Giacomo stopped to look up. A couple of soldiers at the entrance were setting more barriers to guide whoever was coming to this sketchy area in the city.

***

Major Schmidt decided to read Hilda's letter before the making the call to Berlin. He wanted to start the day off in a good mood. He was about to start reading when the phone rang in the secretary's office.

"Herr Major, your car is ready when you are ready to leave," said Marta.

The major didn't answer his secretary, instead continuing with his letter as he drank his strong German coffee. Hilda always started her letters simply, stating that she missed him. This one was no different, and was shorter than most and to the point. She was looking forward to her visit in the spring, and the hospital was busy with German soldiers who needed care. The major smiled, thinking of his beautiful nurse and how she had cared so diligently for him.

"I'm going down to the ghetto to see how it's progressing," the major told Marta as he exited his office, grabbing his jacket and hat.

***

As Gino and Giacomo made their way back to the main street, the purpose of the electrical lines became apparent. Giacomo was getting ready to lift the last pole when a sedan pulled up next to the railroad station.

"Stop what you're doing. I want to see what this is all about," Giacomo said.

Gino stopped working and looked toward the railroad station. As the driver got out of the sedan to let the major out, a junior officer in charge of the railroad area arrived to greet his immediate supervisor. The two saluted.

"Herr Major, we have removed all the residents as you requested. We are waiting for the train to arrive." The young lieutenant walked beside the limping Major Schmidt as the major inspected the way station. The major stopped in front of the crowd corralled behind barriers. Heading toward his next stop, he heard someone yelling.

"You can't load us like cattle and ship us off to another city!"

The major stopped in his tracks. Without saying a word, he turned to see a small, upset man pressing his body against a barrier.

"I want to talk to whoever is in charge!" yelled the man, who was looking at the major.

Schmidt grabbed his head as if he was in pain and looked in the direction of the visibly angry man. Just behind the angry man was a group of about ten other men wondering what was about to happen to their makeshift leader.

"Lieutenant Muller, escort this individual inside the train station so he can meet with the officer that is in charge of this operation," ordered the major.

Lieutenant Muller, who had just reported to Rome from Berlin, wasn't going to let this small Jew make the major look bad. He and a sergeant moved the barrier so the man could come with them. The major continued his walk toward the ghetto while the lieutenant and the sergeant escorted the angry man to the other side of the train station.

"Where are they taking the guy?" asked Gino.

"I don't know, but the major is headed in our direction, so we need to look busy," answered Giacomo, grabbing the last pole to put into position.

Gino helped his friend finish setting the pole as the major walked by them. There was no time to salute since they had their hands wrapped around the final pole.

"Okay, hold that while I get the wedges and bracket."

Giacomo held the pole and looked at the train station. The lieutenant emerged from the station, but without the angry man, and he was in a hurry to catch up with the major. Gino placed the last bracket and wedges in place, and the lieutenant passed by them.

"Where's the guy?" asked Gino.

"I don't know, but I don't think he's coming back anytime soon," said Giacomo, staring at the lieutenant.

The train approached.

"Herr Major, we have blocked off this section of the neighborhood," Lieutenant Muller said. "Once the Gypsies and Jews arrive, they will have nowhere else to go until they are loaded up for their journey to the Motherland."

The major continued without acknowledging what the lieutenant said. "What about the lights? Are there enough lights at night? And can we provide more power if we need additional electricity?"

"We have extended the lights up to the alleyway where they'll be entering at night."

The major inspected the alleyway lights.

"You will need more lights in this area." He pointed at the check-in area. "I also want them extended through all the alleyways in this ghetto so we can see what they are doing at night."

"Yes, Major."

The train stopped past the station house. The sergeant came out by himself. Gino and Giacomo were finishing the last light when they heard a commotion in the train area. German soldiers had opened the doors to livestock and freight cars.

"Nobody is saying anything or objecting to getting on the train," remarked Gino.

"I think they all figured out that if they say anything, they will be escorted to the same place as that fellow who hasn't come back," answered Giacomo.

The group of the men who were taunting the missing man to speak for the group were the first to get on the freight car, without hesitation. A half hour later, all the corralled individuals were loaded. As the train left the station, Gino and Giacomo finished their last light and were ready to hook power to see if all the lights worked.

"I'm going to finish hooking up the power. When I give you the signal, push the switch up to see if all the lights come on," ordered Gino.

As Gino made his way to the connection area down from the alleyway, Giacomo heard people leaving the alley and turned toward the noise. Looking in his direction was the major, with the lieutenant next to him. Giacomo didn't move a muscle as they walked toward the train station.

Gino yelled, "Okay, give it a try!"

The major stopped when he heard the yelling. He saw the large Italian soldier lift a switch, and the lights came on instantly and without any issues. After observing this additional accomplishment to report to his superiors, he continued toward his awaiting sedan with his head held a little higher.

Gino jumped on his big friend in excitement that the lights all came on without problems. But Giacomo wasn't as excited.

"Now, that is what I call good work," remarked Gino. Giacomo looked at the train station. There, for the whole world to see, two German soldiers carried the protestor's limp body out of the train station. They loaded his body into the back of the waiting troop transporter and climbed in. The sergeant looked in their direction, and Giacomo and the sergeant seemed to have a staring-down contest. Gino grabbed his belligerent friend and pulled him away. The sergeant continued to smile as he made his way toward the passenger side of the troop transporter. Sergeant Braun continued to stare at Giacomo even as he entered the troop transporter. He wasn't enjoying his time in Rome but had served under Major Schmidt since the war started. After the major recovered from his wounds, Braun requested duty with the major and regretted that decision. Life in Rome was boring; plus, he detested the Italians. He wanted to be back on front line.

"That asshole, he just stood there looking at me like he wanted me to do something. I should have walked over there and beat on him," said Giacomo.

Gino wasn't in any mood for problems as this day ended.

"Giacomo, you can barely stand straight without any pain, and besides, you only have one good eye. You will have your day. How about we call this a day and head to the pick-up area?"

They picked up their tools when the troop transport took off in the direction opposite the sedan.

As they waited for their transport to take them back to the barracks, Gino noticed the little lieutenant inspecting the lights that led to the clearing. After the officer was done, he wrote something in a small notebook he drew out of his pocket.

What is he writing down? thought Gino.

His attention shifted as the troop transport pulled up to gather all the Italian soldiers working in the ghetto. It was already half full of soldiers from other sites. Most were ditchdiggers or helping out at construction sites. They were of little use due to their wounds, but the military leaders refused to let them out of the army.

Gino and Giacomo were sitting on the ground when the transport pulled up. They got up and noticed the lieutenant hand a note to the German soldier in the passenger seat. The workers were told the German soldier was there for their protection, but most of them knew he was present to make sure none of them deserted. He was the only one with a gun, and none of them wanted to get shot.

Once they were all loaded, the transport headed back to their barracks; the ghetto was the last stop of the day.

"I guess the Germans are in charge now," remarked Giacomo as he sat next to his friend.

"It would seem so, my friend, but we still take orders from our army."

They held onto the upper bars of the transport as it rumbled on. They disembarked in front of the barracks. Gino and Giacomo were the last ones to get out. As they exited, their Italian senior enlisted approached the front cab. The German soldier's arm extended, holding the same piece of paper Lieutenant Muller handed him earlier. Sergeant Sal did not say a word before he headed for the Italian officer barracks on the other side of the road.

"I guess we have our work assignments for tomorrow," remarked Giacomo as he entered their open-bay barracks. Gino smiled and followed his friend to some well-deserved rest and hopefully their one hot meal of the day.

Chapter 10

GETTING READY IN THE open-bay barracks was always a challenge. With so many soldiers living in one room, everyone wanted the same thing at the same time, which never worked out. Saturdays and Sundays were the only days that they enjoyed a meal sent by their superiors. They had to fend for themselves during the week. Saturday was a day of work but usually filled with tasks like cleaning or other less physical jobs. Sunday was the only day that the Italian workers enjoyed off, but they still had to muster in the morning and evening.

Gino was up before most of the other soldiers and ready for work when the food arrived. He waited for Giacomo. Both were tired and in need of rest as they moved toward the large vat of smoking mystery pasta.

"I need to go home again and see if my mother is alive," remarked Gino.

"Then go back home. I'll cover for you. Just make sure you come back by Sunday night," answered Giacomo.

"It would take all day just to get there. Then I'd have to come back in a few short hours."

"If my mother was missing, I would want to know if she were alive, especially if there was no one to take care of her. You already lost your father and brothers. Go find out if your mother is alive. If you get caught, there is no one but your mother that they will go after. You still have the shoe salesman suitcase from the last time you went. Use that ploy again."

Gino had stored the suitcase under their table in the barracks with the other contraband. He could get Giacomo to distract everyone, get the suitcase and head for the train station for the noon train going north.

"I'm going. Distract everyone so I can get the suitcase. See you back here on Sunday night."

"Good luck, my friend. Tell Catherina I said hello."

Gino was moving before Giacomo finished the sentence. Within a minute he was at the table with his jacket and hat ready. Gino watched Giacomo move toward the vat for his morning food. Just about everyone was either in line or eating when he heard his giant friend's first words.

"What kind of food is this you're feeding us this morning? We work our asses off all week for this crap! I bet the Germans are being fed better than us."

Giacomo threw his plate down to make his point. As the food settled on the floor, out came Sergeant Sal from his one-room office and bunk.

Sergeant Sal walked with a limp and had only one arm. Nobody knew where he had been wounded, only that he was always in a bad mood and hated the Germans.

"What is going on here, Private Romano?" demanded the sergeant.

Giacomo looked over Sal's head to see Gino and saw the table in the tilted position through the rows of bunks. He needed to continue his uproar longer.

"Sergeant, look at this watered-down, soupy pasta they serve us. I bet the Germans are eating better than we are. We don't even get bread with this pasta. What kind of Italian serves pasta without bread?"

Sal looked at the mess on the floor, then shifted his attention to the vat and the workers serving the food.

"Where is the bread that I requested with this meal?" asked the sergeant.

"This is all they gave us to serve this morning, Sergeant."

"Private Romano, clean up this mess or I'll have you put in

the barracks jail."

Giacomo was about to launch into another rage when he noticed Gino slipping through the exit with the suitcase under his jacket.

"No problem, Sergeant." He retrieved the cleaning supplies. Sergeant Sal went back into his office, but not for long. He emerged with his hat and headed out to find out where the rest of the food was going.

Gino made the switch to salesman as soon as he cleared the barracks. Getting around the city on a Saturday proved to be no problem, especially if you were not wearing a uniform. Since arriving in Rome, he had learned not to board trains at the main station. The main stations were the ones being watched by the authorities. If you wanted to leave Rome without being noticed, you needed to board trains at smaller stations and switch trains later in the journey. With little effort, he was on his way out of Rome, heading back home in search of his mother.

After switching trains in Florence and Venice, Gino arrived in Pordenone early in the evening. With little time to spare, he purchased a one-way ticket back to the Rome before leaving the station in search of his mother. He would deal with what Rome had to offer the next day. As he left the station, he spotted a farm truck heading out of the city toward his family farm. He waved at the driver, who just pointed to the rear, which already had passengers. After throwing the suitcase in the back, he joined the other hitchhikers. Gino sat at the end of the truck, looking back with his hat lowered and coat covering most of his face. If the truck kept this pace, he would be home in about twenty minutes.

Gino noticed that the terrain looked horrible as they left the city. All of the majestic trees that once lined the roads were long gone; just the stumps remained. Most of the houses and farms looked abandoned. He worried that his childhood home would be another casualty of war. Looking right, he soon saw the distant house in the middle of his childhood playground field. Without raising any suspicion, he kept looking to the rear of the truck just in case someone recognized the farm and him. After they had passed several other homes and farms, he jumped off the truck and went the opposite direction. Within minutes the truck was out of sight and he was on the other side of the road heading for the farm. The field was overgrown with weeds that he did not recognize but they gave him great cover.

It was close to evening muster when Giacomo noticed that everyone was moving toward the front of the barracks. Giacomo surveyed the room and waited at the exit for the sergeant. When the last soldier left the barracks, the sergeant came out with his muster sheet in hand.

"Sergeant Sal, I want to apologize for this morning," remarked Giacomo. He smelled the wine on the Sal's breath.

"Private Romano, you need to control that temper of yours before someone takes out your other eye."

"You are correct. It won't happen again. Do you want me to take muster for you so you don't have to go out in the cold?"

Sal looked at the overgrown soldier for a minute. Then he handed him the muster sheet. "Let me know if anybody is missing. I'll be in my room."

"No problem, Sergeant," smiled Giacomo as he exited the barracks.

***

Dim light came from the main house and smoke rose from the lone chimney. The light was hard to see through the cloudy, solitary window on the side. Moving to the back, he noticed that just about all the farming gear was gone, but a motorcycle leaned against the house. There were no animals and the small barn in the back was about to collapse. Gino took a deep breath before opening the back door. Soon he was looking into the eyes of his cousin Maurizio.

"Gino, is that you?"

"Maurizio, what are you doing here?"

Maurizio stood with a cane and was missing half of his right leg. Before saying another word, they hugged one another.

"What happened to your leg, where is my mother, and what are you doing here?"

Maurizio moved slightly away from Gino before replying, "Your mother is in France with my family. The Germans came looking for her after they killed your father. She was able to get away before they arrived. I was in Egypt when I lost my leg and they discharged me. This was the only place left standing when I returned from the war. I'm taking care of the farm until she returns."

"Can you take me to the Zucchet Farm? I need to see my family before I head back to Rome tomorrow."

"If you don't mind riding on a motorcycle, we can be there in fifteen minutes."

Pietro was sitting outside the farmhouse enjoying his evening smoke and coffee when he saw the lone headlight coming toward the farm.

"Bruno, come out. We have a visitor coming."

Bruno heard his father from the kitchen and headed outside to be by his side. As soon as he made his way through the door, he could see the headlight coming toward the farmhouse.

"It doesn't look like a German motorcycle, and there are two people," remarked Bruno as the light got brighter.

The motorcycle made the left into the driveway leading to the farmhouse. Pietro threw his cigarette on the ground as he rose for their unexpected visitors.

"It's Maurizio, but I don't know who's in the back," remarked Bruno.

"It's Gino. I recognize the bag," said Pietro.

"What are you doing here?" asked Bruno as the motorcycle came to a stop in front of the farmhouse.

Gino stepped off the motorcycle and replied, "I needed to check on my mother and I was hoping to see Catherina and Maria before I go back tomorrow."

"Of course, you can see them. Catherina is upstairs putting Maria down for the evening. Maurizio, you come in as well and have some wine and food."

Gino was heading inside when he heard a loud noise from the house and out came Catherina to greet her husband.

"I heard your voice from the upstairs window."

"Everyone go inside before someone sees Gino," ordered Pietro.

***

Bruno waited for the express train. It was the first of the day and the only one going to Rome. This train would only make a few stops before its final stop in Rome. Gino stood next to the lobby exit waiting for the signal from Bruno. If there were any issues, he would bolt and head for the woods.

The train was already five minutes late when Bruno noticed Fascist supporters waiting for the same train. Bruno moved to the end of the tracks. He wanted to put some space in between them and Gino. Just as he made it to the other end, he heard the train coming into the station.

Where did Bruno go? thought Gino as the train rolled to a stop.

With only a minute to spare, Bruno walked away from the tracks. Within seconds he stood next to Gino.

"Head toward the back of that passenger car. There are supporters on the other car. Good luck."

Gino headed toward the tracks, not taking his eyes off the passenger car in front of him. He boarded and took a seat at the end. The train soon headed off for the southwest part of Italy. After leaving the station, Gino raised his head to assess the situation. There were a few passengers, but none that concerned him. He rose and spotted the familiar brown jackets of Mussolini supporters in the next car. There was nothing he could do but sit with his head down low and hopefully get back to his unit before being missed.

On Sunday morning the barracks was about empty when Giacomo started looking for a substitute for Gino. Luckily, he and Gino were always in the back for muster, which made it easy to conceal them from the roll call. Standing about two rows from him was a good substitute for Gino. He moved quickly toward the unsuspecting soldier. Sergeant Sal was always the last to emerge from the barracks to start the muster, and today would be no different.

"After you answer your name in the roll call, move in the back next to me to answer for Cartelli," Giacomo whispered to the soldier that was about the same height as his missing friend.

"No problem, but I want two packs of cigarettes for my troubles," he answered.

"Deal, but if you screw this up, you'll be needing a patch for one of your eyes."

The sergeant emerged from the empty barracks barely awake

and only slightly in regulation uniform. He started yelling names before he even came to a stop in front of the muster. Before long, the soldier who agreed to answer for cigarettes had answered his name. The other soldiers moved out of his way so he could stand next to Giacomo. In less than a minute, the soldier answered for Cartelli, the muster was over and everyone was dismissed for the rest of their day off.

The train was almost to Rome when Gino looked at his watch. If he moved very quickly, he could make the evening muster once they arrived. As the train slowed down for their final stop, Gino noticed Germans all over the tracks looking in the train cars. He started to sweat; if he was the first to depart, he probably would be noticed. The forward car emptied out. The Germans greeted the brown jackets as they exited.

For a moment, Gino relaxed, until he noticed two German leather-jacketed men headed in his direction from the forward car. They were stopping everyone left on the passenger cars. Gino grabbed his bag and headed through the doors connecting the passenger car to the coal car. He quickly changed out of his suit and into his uniform without even looking to see who was watching. After throwing the suitcase into the pile of coal, he exited the train and the station without looking back.

The barracks was full of soldiers getting out of the cold weather when Gino arrived. He was chilly and still full of adrenaline when he saw Giacomo sitting in their corner lounge reading a paper.

"I'm back. Did I miss anything?"

Giacomo didn't even put down the paper to look at him. He just said, "You owe me three packs of cigarettes. How was your visit?"

Chapter 11

THE MORNINGS IN ROME were always the same. After the ringing of bells from countless churches, everyone in the Italian barracks made their way toward their mustering station, where they would receive their daily work assignments.

Gino was already at his assigned spot. He looked around at everyone in their normal places. He smiled sarcastically because it was a crowd of broken-down human beings. Almost every person was either missing a part of their body or couldn't stand straight.

Are we that desperate we have to use our wounded to fix our cities? thought Gino.

As he finished looking around, he felt Giacomo's left forearm on his shoulder.

"What are you smirking about?" Giacomo asked.

Giacomo was always a little late due to his size and difficulty getting around in the morning. He was tucking in his shirt with his right hand, but that wasn't what made Gino laugh at him.

"Now what's so funny?"

Gino pointed at his shoes. Giacomo looked down; they were unlaced and on the wrong feet.

"Damn it, I thought there was something wrong with my shoes, but the feeling in my legs takes a while to get going in the morning."

Gino reached down to help his friend out, knowing Giacomo couldn't switch his shoes without sitting. After a couple of minutes, Giacomo's shoes were ready for the day.

"What is taking so long for the sergeant to come out?" asked Gino.

"Look," remarked Giacomo.

Gino couldn't see as far as Giacomo, but he looked toward the area where he was pointing to see what caught his attention. There was the little German lieutenant coming out of the Italian officer's barracks. As he exited the barracks, he got into a sedan that was waiting for him. The sedan rolled toward the ghetto area of the city. After a couple of minutes, Sergeant Sal emerged from the barracks with their daily work assignments.

After each soldier's name was called they went to separate staging areas to await transportation. Gino and Giacomo didn't pay too much attention to the assignments since they figured they would be going back to the ghetto to finish the lights. As they headed to the toolshed, they noticed some of the soldiers whispering to one another and staring at Giacomo. Gino ignored the whispers as he inventoried the tools he had accumulated since coming to Rome. Stares were not unusual due to Giacomo's huge size and eye patch. Most soldiers would come for only a week or so before being cleared for further duties. This made for new faces on a daily basis; the turnover rate for the Italian soldiers was quick. The soldiers' whispers were a sign of anxiety and uncertainty.

The two friends settled in with the other soldiers going to the ghetto. After each soldier went to their area, the sergeant made a quick tour to ensure they were in the right place.

"Private Romano, you're in the wrong group," yelled Sal. The sergeant pointed at the group of soldiers who regularly did digging. Most of the work was at the granite mines of *Fosse Ardeatine.*

"See you later," Giacomo said.

They must have something big to move today, thought Gino as his friend left.

"What are we moving today?" asked Giacomo. No one answered; in fact, most of the soldiers moved away from him as he got closer.

This can't be good, he thought.

The troop transports made their stops. As the troop transport drove toward the ghetto, Gino looked out the back. His friend's transport was directly behind his and made the turn to the granite mines. He smiled sympathetically; his huge friend was going to have a tough day moving dirt in the sun.

Gino's transport stopped to let everyone out. He jumped down with what tools he'd managed to appropriate over time. He smelled human waste. There was little of that yesterday, but today it was if someone had opened a door or hatch to let this horrible smell out. He held his shirt over his nose, but it didn't help. As he walked toward the same area as before, he inspected the electrical lines and lights to make sure everything was still in working order. All the connections were in good shape. Gino carried what electrical wiring he had left past the check-in area. Next to the check-in area, a fire smoldered. That was where the odor was the strongest. While he looked for an area to construct the new run, he heard some soldiers speaking German on the main road. Lieutenant Muller talked with the sergeant who was at the train station yesterday.

I wonder what they did with that body from the train station, he thought. Then he realized what must have been in the fire. Without giving them a second look, Gino worked the new electrical line toward the ghetto alley and listened to the German discussion. The noisy morning made it difficult to hear their conversation.

"Remember what the major said, Sergeant Braun. Try not to kill the soldier. Just teach him a lesson. We need them and don't want to start a revolt with our fellow Axis partners," ordered the lieutenant.

"Where is he?"

"He's down the road at the granite mines. Look for the holes in the field as you drive toward the barracks. Don't do anything until later on. Let everything settle in before you start beating the soldier. You always want to make sure no one sees you and pick soldiers who will not talk. If you want to get a message out to the other workers, use a person that will set an example and show we are in control. In this situation, the biggest soldier will do the trick."

The sergeant smiled at the lieutenant before he turned and headed to the sedan.

The smell from the fire bothered Gino. He dropped the electrical wiring and went to the empty buildings, retreating into the inner workings of the alleyways to get relief. There was some, but now his nose filled with a mix of ash and decay from the old granite buildings. The walls were cold and wet from being built too close to one another, blocking the sun and inviting dampness. As Gino continued through the buildings, it became apparent that something was missing from each house—windows, doors and flooring.

He quickly realized the soldiers removed all the wood from the structures. That would have been one of the reasons for the fire. Granite, brick, or rocks remained in all of the buildings. The flooring was also removed. Even his barracks had wooden floors to get some relief from the bitterness of the elements. He had never seen anything like this before and felt lucky to not be living in such conditions. This made the task of hanging the wiring even more difficult. He needed more wooden poles, but there were none, so he had to use the walls to hang the wiring and lights. This would require some type of metal spikes to be used to hang the wiring, and of course he had none.

***

Giacomo was immediately unsure about his new work assignment. As the dust settled from the truck, he let everyone get out first. Just to make sure he had a chance of getting out of this alive, he armed himself with a shovel. After a couple of minutes, he heard everyone heading to their designated area to begin work. He jumped from the rear of the transport and immediately fell to his knees from the severe back pain. Giacomo regained his composure and saw the driver and German soldier having a cigarette. Both looked in his direction with puzzled expressions as they puffed on their lighted sticks. The German soldier nodded toward the other ditchdiggers.

Giacomo lowered the shovel and slowly walked to the day's work of dust, dirt, and rock. He approached the ditch, which was the foundation of a building that had yet to be constructed. Other buildings had been erected, so his concern that this was a big grave was laid to rest. He looked at the other soldiers stretched in all directions before he began the long, slow descent into the ditch. Getting on his knees first, then onto his stomach so he could turn his legs into the ditch, was the only way to manage the descent with as little pain as possible. Once in the ditch, he would need help to get out, which meant at least two other soldiers assisting him. Giacomo approached some of the other soldiers before getting to the task of moving the earth.

"How long do we do this for?" asked Giacomo, stabbing his shovel into the dirt.

"We usually work until they come by with some water and a piece of bread," answered one of the workers.

He thanked the soldier for his answer and proceeded to dig in silence.

***

"You there, why haven't you started to hang more lights?" yelled Muller.

Gino turned around to see the skinny lieutenant looking in his direction.

"I'm looking for some way to hang the lights since we have no more poles."

The lieutenant looked at the walls for a minute. "Come with me."

They went to the fire area, which made Gino put his shirt over his nose and mouth. The fire was about out and mostly ash.

"Look in the fire and see if any metal survived that you can use to hang the lights."

Gino halted, knowing he was going to have to dig through whatever horrors lay in this fire pit of war.

***

Dust settled into Giacomo's hair, nose, and most of his other body parts. His back was throbbing and even his eye patch hurt. The day could not end sooner. As he stopped to wipe the sweat off of his brow, dead silence caught his attention. He was the only one in the pit.

Where did everyone else go? They're probably getting their afternoon meal, thought Giacomo.

Getting out of this pit wasn't going to happen without somebody helping, so he continued digging until they came back. Punching his shovel into the soil, he heard a sedan pull up but was too deep to see who was in the sedan or what was about to happen.

As the sedan pulled in, most of the Italian soldiers had already made their distance from the intended target. The only one near the ditch was the German guard who was making sure the objective wasn't going anywhere. When the dust settled from the sedan, the doors opened to reveal four soldiers.

"Where is he?" asked Braun, rolling up his sleeves along with the other soldiers. The German soldier moved out of the way and pointed to the ditch next to him.

Giacomo heard footsteps on the other side of the ditch. He turned, expecting his countrymen back from their break, but to his surprise there weren't any Italians in view. Instead, he saw the sergeant from the train station with some other Germans at the ridge of the ditch. Giacomo was perplexed at first, thinking they were going to help him dig, but that thought soon passed. He shifted his grip on the shovel. The sergeant was the first to drop into the ditch, followed by the three large soldiers. Giacomo shifted so he could protect his only eye but still inflict some damage to his attackers.

"Private, put the shovel down and we'll take it easy on you," ordered Braun.

Giacomo smiled, knowing no matter what he did this wasn't going to go well for him. He lowered the shovel for a moment and one of the German soldiers rushed him. Giacomo smashed the soldier with the back of the shovel. A cloud of dust erupted as the other three soldiers rushed the giant Italian. Giacomo held the shovel in front of his face to protect his only good eye before the punches and kicks pummeled his body. He fell to his stomach and curled into the fetal position, keeping the shovel over his head. Just when he thought the worst was over, a huge weight landed on him. His back snapped loudly before he passed out from the pain.

"That is enough," yelled the sergeant. Braun grabbed

Giacomo's shovel but couldn't get him to release it. Releasing the shovel, Braun dusted off his trousers and ordered, "Let's go. He's done for the day."

***

After looking around the huge firepit, Gino found a metal rod for poking and numerous metal spikes used to hang shutters and windows. He also found bones deep in the middle. That was the source of the horrible smell. Gino couldn't tell whether the remains were human or animal, and he didn't want to know. He continued to search for metal spikes, concentrating on the outer ring. All the spikes were still hot. He placed them on the edge of the fire to cool. Having rescued various types of spikes, he rushed to get as far away as possible from the odor burning his nose raw. After getting back to his electrical wire, he examined the spikes closely. Most were usable, but a few were beyond the trouble.

Starting at one end of the narrow alleyway, he punched the spikes into the walls. He only had an old chair available, so raising the wiring to any reasonable height was a challenge. Gino even went inside the apartments to drive some of the spikes into the outer walls. As the workday ended, he hung the lights as quickly as possible. The Germans wanted everything done, but with only himself to hang the lights, he would need more than a day.

Gino heard the transport pull up. He stopped what he was doing to grab a seat back home. As he cleared the ghetto, he heard Lieutenant Muller.

"Where are you going? Come here."

Gino saw the German on the other side of the fire of death.

"Herr Lieutenant, if I don't get on that transport, I will not be able to get back to the barracks tonight."

"Are you done hanging the lights?"

"I was the only one hanging lights today. If my electrical partner was with me, we would have finished stringing them. I need another day to finish."

There was about a minute of silence while the German took notes and looked around the ghetto. Gino fidgeted, waiting for the officer to give him permission to leave.

"Private, you may go, and make sure you finish tomorrow with whatever partner you get, or you won't be leaving until you're done."

Gino saluted and turned to his ride home. As he jumped in the back of the transport Gino thought, *What did he mean "whatever partner I get"?*

***

The ditch the Germans soldiers used as their beating ground a few hours earlier was quiet. The only visible sign of a human being was two hands holding a wooden handle and boots sticking out of the dirt. No one had dared to go back into the hole after the Germans departed some three hours ago. Everyone was scared to go look at what was left of their Italian giant. All four Germans looked like they had been in a battle with a bear. If they looked that bad, one could only imagine what was left of their fellow soldier.

Giacomo opened his eye—it was working, which was a surprise. He thought after that beating he might end up blind. His head pounded from the blade of the shovel wedged against his head. The long wooden handle was underneath his armpit and pressed against his body. He moved his arm to release the pressure, and within seconds the pounding in his head subsided.

Why am I under all this dirt? Giacomo wondered as he moved his legs.

Gino was still in the back of the transport thinking about what the lieutenant said to him, and with one deep breath, he figured it out—something was going to happen to Giacomo. He glanced out the back to see where the transport was on the road heading to the barracks.

Have we gone by the granite mines yet?

He scanned the landscape to the left. They were approaching the ditches. He squinted and saw the broken-down Italian troops loading on the transport. He looked inside the transport, knowing Giacomo always sat in the front. Between the road dust and the movement of the truck carrying him, Gino could barely see. They were about parallel to the other transport when Gino determined there was no sign of Giacomo. Something happened to his friend.

After rolling out of the dirt, Giacomo was on his back. Most of his exterior injuries were minor—cuts and bruises to his head and arms. He had trouble breathing from some bruised or broken ribs. That must have been the snap he heard when he passed out. What puzzled him was that the back pain he had felt since the battle in Greece wasn't there anymore. *Probably because I have so many other injuries the old ones cannot compete.*

Giacomo's attention went from his injuries to what he was hearing. A lot of noise came from the road near the ditches. It sounded as though the soldiers were loading and heading out from the day's work. He had a hard time getting up, and every time he tried to yell the pain from his chest stopped him. All he could muster was a whisper. Giacomo rolled on his left side, grabbing the shovel and getting to his knees. He heard the transport pull away. With the only strength he could gather, the giant threw the shovel out of the hole before falling onto his stomach.

Gino stood scanning the work field for his friend. He ignored commands to sit. The other transport pulled out of the field and onto the dirt road. As the transport turned right, a shovel popped out of one of the ditches.

"Did you see that?"

Nobody even looked in Gino's direction. If he jumped from the transport, he could be shot for desertion. Without wasting another minute, Gino jumped and hit the road just clear of the next truck in the caravan. Only the Italian soldiers next to Gino noticed. No one so much as blinked; desertions happened about every day in Rome.

The transport's Italian driver saw Gino jump. He glanced at the German guard sitting next to him, but the German had already closed his eyes for the ride home. Having witnessed what happened to Giacomo earlier in the day, the driver didn't say a word to the guard.

Giacomo heard the transport drive away. For a moment of silence, all he heard was the distant noise of the trucks.

"Damn it. How am I going to get out of this ditch?" whispered Giacomo as he rolled to his back in pain.

Gino ran to the nearest pile of rocks to hide. After sitting for a minute or two and watching both trucks head for the barracks, he finally caught his breath. Gino rushed the hole as quickly as possible to avoid being seen. He grabbed the shovel before jumping in, just in case he needed protection.

Giacomo was trying to regain the strength to get to his feet when he heard someone running in his direction. He tried to get on his knees to regain some type of defensive position and was stunned by the individual who landed in the hole. He looked at the faded gray uniform and couldn't believe his eyes.

"How did you know I was in this hole?"

Gino stared at his friend. "I didn't, but you weren't on the transport and the lieutenant said something that made me think you were in danger. When I saw the shovel being thrown out of the hole, I knew there was someone here. You look like someone beat you senseless."

Giacomo laughed and the sharp pain in his chest made him keel over.

"Okay, what's broken, and, more importantly, can you walk?" Gino grabbed the giant's shoulders to prop him up and assess his wounds. "What is hurting, my friend?"

"Well, I think some ribs might be broken or at least bruised because it is hard to breathe or talk. My head feels like it's going to explode from the pounding it took, but that's all."

"Can you get on your feet? How is your back?"

"Ugh!" yelled Giacomo as Gino assisted him to his feet to ascertain how bad it was.

"Well, can you walk?"

"Walking won't be the problem. Getting out of this ditch will be the issue."

Gino chuckled as he wiped dirt from his friend.

"We are going to have to figure something out, but not until it gets dark. You need to sit down and rest before someone sees that big head of yours sticking out of this hole," said Gino. He put his arm around Giacomo to help him back down to a resting position.

***

As the transports turned into the barracks compound, Sergeant Sal was waiting to take muster as he had over and over again since arriving in Rome after losing his arm in battle. He was the only authority for the night; the other Italian officers usually went home before the soldiers arrived back to the barracks. The Italian soldiers climbed out of the transports and headed for the muster area. They always took muster when they got back from their work detail and before being dismissed for the evening. The sergeant waited patiently as all the soldiers took their places in line. As the sergeant yelled out names, the transport pulled away, back to the truck pool area. Sal went down his list, and when he got to Gino Cartelli's name there was silence and some whispering from the other soldiers.

He called again, "Gino Cartelli!" but there was nothing but whispering.

The sergeant looked in the back and saw two empty spaces where his electricians usually stood. He didn't bother to call Giacomo's name.

"Fall out!" yelled Sal after the muster was over.

He looked around as the men went their separate ways. Some of the soldiers went to eat while others went to their sleeping quarters for some well-deserved rest. The sergeant headed over to the toolshed, which was his responsibility to lock at night. He took a quick look inside; the electrician tools and one shovel were missing.

Damn it. I'm going to have to tell the lieutenant we don't have any electricians in the morning, he thought.

***

As night fell, Gino got a little nervous about their situation. *How am I going to get my friend out of this ditch?* he thought.

"Wake up," Gino whispered to Giacomo, who had fallen asleep about an hour ago. "How are you doing?"

"I'm fine. The pounding in my head has stopped, but it's still hard to breathe," answered Giacomo. He used the side of the ditch to sit up.

"Stay here," Gino said as he climbed out of the hole.

Gino searched the area for anything that could help his friend. As Giacomo sat looking up at the stars, a rope uncoiled down into the hole. Gino jumped back in.

"The rope is the only thing around here. You have any ideas?"

"What's on the other end of this rope?"

"Oh, it's tied to a tree. Don't worry; it will hold you, I think."

They laughed as Gino helped Giacomo to his feet. He grabbed the rope with both hands and pulled hard to make sure it was holding.

"Ugh, this is going to hurt," Giacomo said.

"I have an idea. What if I get on my hands and knees and you step on top of me and pull yourself out of the hole?"

"It might work, but can you take all of my weight?"

"We will have to see, but let's give this a try."

Giacomo and Gino got into position.

"You ready?" asked Giacomo.

"Yes, let's do this, and don't hurt me."

Giacomo put his left boot on Gino's back and, with one good thrust, pushed to the top of the ditch as he pulled the rope with both hands. His body accelerated until he was almost out of the hole. Gino pushed from the bottom, which helped him clear the hole. Gino heard another "ugh" and looked up to see the bottoms of Giacomo's boots.

"You okay?"

"Yes, I'm fine. Let's get back to the barracks so I can get something to eat."

"You're always hungry. Let's go before they decide to come look for us."

They arrived under the cover of darkness about an hour later. Gino noticed Giacomo was walking better than expected after such a beating. Giacomo also hadn't complained about his back, which surprised Gino. They were able to wash up, grab some leftover dinner, and head to their bunks.

The next morning, Gino was getting out of his bunk when he saw Giacomo for the first time in the light.

"You look like someone took a stick and hit your face a bunch of times. Since when can you bend over and tie your shoes?"

"Since they jumped on my back and snapped something back in place."

"You want me to jump on your face to fix what they did yesterday?"

Giacomo smiled and waited for Gino to get ready.

Sergeant Sal sat in the main building adjacent to the barracks waiting for the Italian officer, who was always running late, before he went out and took the morning muster. He didn't want to tell the officer that Gino Cartelli and Giacomo Romano went missing, which meant they would need two more electricians to finish the work the Germans wanted completed. Ten minutes past muster time, the sergeant decided to take roll call and notify the officer of the missing soldiers when he finally arrived.

Gino and Giacomo took their places in the back. They were accustomed to stares from the other soldiers, but this morning there seemed to be a more celebratory atmosphere. Most of the soldiers looking in their direction were smiling, with the occasional grin.

"Are you seeing this?" asked Gino.

"See what? The only thing I'm doing is trying to stand straight so I don't let the Germans know I'm in pain."

Gino grinned as the sedans pulled up.

As Sal stepped outside, he saw Colonel Specca pull up with the always-present Germans. He approached the Italian officer to give him a brief and, of course, to get his work detail guidance from the Germans.

"What kind of great news do you have for us this morning, Sergeant?" asked the Italian officer in charge.

Sergeant Sal moved his only arm to retrieve a written report in his pocket for his superiors, when he decided to look at the men to his left. To his surprise, there they both were standing and looking in his direction with smirks. He could not miss the big head with an eye patch towering over the other soldiers, and neither could the other officers. They all looked at the men simultaneously.

"I have nothing to report, sir, except that I have to take morning muster to make sure all the men are here."

Gino whispered to Giacomo, "Is the soldier next to the sedan the one who did this to you?"

Giacomo aimed his one eye at the sedan. "Him and three others."

Gino smiled. Nobody expected Giacomo to be here, but here he was, and this would send a message to the Germans not to mess with the Italians.

As the German walked toward the awaiting sedan, he

stopped before getting in. "The big Italian is here. I thought you hurt him yesterday," Lieutenant Muller remarked to Braun, who held the door open for him. The German sergeant looked over his right shoulder into the crowd of soldiers to see one soldier in back towering over everyone.

How is this possible? We left him unconscious under a mound of dirt yesterday, thought Braun. He couldn't believe what he was seeing. He moved to the driver side of the sedan, but not before looking at Giacomo and Gino one more time.

"Attention to muster," yelled Sergeant Sal, who was smiling along with his superior officer. They looked at Giacomo knowing this would be a good day.

Chapter 12

ROME WASN'T THE MOST pleasant place during the winter of 1941. With all of the violence and desertions, the Germans ran the city with little resistance from Italy's Fascist Party. The Fascist members had become mere translators with little or no authority over their own citizens or troops.

Most of the Italian army regulars were shipped out to fight the Axis powers' battles, which were not going well, especially in Russia where the Germans had been stalled by the weather and insufficient supplies. For the first time since the war started, the Axis powers experienced defeat. This made their commanders suspicious of everyone unsupportive of their cause. Most of their subordinates felt the pressure as well, which made life difficult for the disabled soldiers in Rome.

**

Gino was freezing as he worked to restore power to a building that had lost its electricity from a downed power line. This winter was extremely harsh and he wasn't getting much sleep. He wondered if transferring to Rome had been the smart thing to do; at least in Naples work wasn't as hectic and the Germans weren't in charge. He did hear that a German division moved into Naples after he departed, though, so maybe he was screwed no matter where he was stationed. Better to be in Rome and closer to his family, although he hadn't been able to visit recently.

Germans kept a close watch on the injured Italians soldiers, increasing animosity. There were more and more desertions from the ranks and open discussions about how poorly the Axis partners treated Italian countrymen. In the past, any talk against Italy's allies would have brought a death sentence, but now it was common to speak out and not be punished. Regular Italian citizens were being punished for helping deserters. This wasn't new, but now most of the punishments were carried out by the Germans soldiers. If you were caught with a deserter in your home, it was a certain death sentence for all who lived in the home.

Gino and the other workers were done for the day, and they all gathered at the pick-up point. As Gino sat waiting for the troop transport, he gazed at his surroundings, and, all of sudden, it hit him.

He was a prisoner in his own army with no hope or future. There was always a German soldier watching them, and they lived in an open-bay barracks while the Germans lived in hotels with their own rooms. Food was scant and he couldn't remember the last time he had any wine. The army started giving him pay vouchers months ago with no promise of ever getting back pay.

As the truck pulled in, Gino's rage grew. He sat next to Giacomo and glanced back at the armed German soldiers guarding them. Most of the workers suffered from unspeakable wounds, and to have their allies treat them like slaves was too much. Gino nudged Giacomo to point out the armed German.

"The Germans treat us like we're the prisoners of war. They don't even pretend to be allies any longer," Gino said to his friend.

The men exited the transport in front of their open-bay barracks. As usual, Giacomo was the last to get out. They hurried inside to get out of the cold and headed for their corner of the barracks to sit in a makeshift lounge of old wooden wire spools. The spools made great tables and the smaller ones could be used as chairs—benefits of being electricians. This place might feel like a prison, but it was home and warm.

"Why is it we have to live in this dump but the Germans get to stay in the hotels?" asked Giacomo.

Gino took his jacket and gloves off as Giacomo did the same and responded, "I wish I knew. It doesn't seem right. This is our country, but they get better living conditions than we do."

Giacomo hung his jacket next to his bunk and grabbed his cards. They would play for about an hour before heading over to the main hall for dinner—typically a bowl of pasta and some bread. As Giacomo dealt, he looked around to make sure they were alone before he spoke. He feared many of the soldiers who lived in the barracks were not trustworthy.

Giacomo looked at his friend and said, "What's on your mind, buddy?"

"Well, I think it's only a matter of time before something happens to us, and it's not going to be good. The Germans don't like Italians. That is obvious by the way they treat us. Probably because of how badly we've been doing in the battles as of late. Or maybe they just see us as yet another inferior race."

"You're right about the way they treat us, we need to keep our *eye* open. Trust no one."

Gino cracked a smile, but he had noticed that Giacomo sometimes looked with both eyes. Gino always thought it was odd. Maybe it was force of habit. *Or maybe . . . could he be faking the injury?* Giacomo usually wore a patch over the bad eye, but when he was playing cards or reading, he often took the patch off. When Gino asked why he removed the patch, Giacomo would say that the patch was putting pressure on his head or the patch was new and it bothered him. Gino laughed as Giacomo moved the patch to the familiar spot above his eye.

"Is that a new eye patch, buddy?"

"You know it's the same patch. What is so funny?"

"Nothing. Is it time to eat yet? I'm starving."

As they prepared to go to dinner, the barracks door opened. The rest of the Italian wounded workers filed in. Most were laborers with no special skills. Their days were filled with moving rocks, digging ditches, clearing trees and chopping and stacking firewood. Many were jealous of the easy jobs of the electricians, fueling Giacomo's suspicions of his fellow Italians.

As they made their way to the front door, a man named

Giorgio ask them where they were going, but Gino and Giacomo ignored him. Giorgio had become increasingly vocal about the living conditions and mistreatment by the Germans and had formed a dissident group that met off the compound. He and others always wanted to know about electrical work so that they too could escape the backbreaking tasks of being a laborer.

Giorgio was playing with fire, and Giacomo had no interest in getting throttled again. As he and Gino were about to leave, someone yelled at them to stop and come back into the barracks for a meeting. It was Sergeant Sal. They disliked him, but they didn't want any trouble, so they complied and took a seat.

"Let me have everyone's attention so we can get this over with and go have some dinner. There has been a lot of open talk about desertion and the overall dislike of our German brothers as of late. The Germans are our allies and we are working with them to make Europe a better place. The Italian Royal Army and Il Duce have given their full support and we need to give them our support as well. Anybody talking about deserting or getting caught trying to desert will be hanged or face a firing squad by the local authorities. We are all in the Italian Royal Army until we win the war in Europe."

About half of the unit applauded and the rest frowned in disbelief. Gino looked at Giacomo and motioned to the door with his head. As they approached to leave, it opened from the other side and they quickly stepped aside.

Two Germans in black-and-red uniforms entered, followed by an Italian officer. Gino quickly looked back through the doorway to see if any other soldiers were coming in. Outside, German and Italian soldiers with guns blocked all camp exits.

Not a good sign, thought Gino as Sergeant Sal called attention.

Colonel Specca, the senior Italian officer in Rome, made his way to the front of the room while the German officers stopped to let him by. The officer gestured to Sergeant Sal to follow him into the conference room.

"What do you think is going on?" Gino asked Giacomo.

"I don't know, but it's not going to be good for someone. If this gets ugly, we need to find a way out of here, and the closest exit is the window to the right. Do you see it?"

Gino nodded.

Sergeant Sal emerged from the room followed by the Italian colonel, who walked over and whispered to the German officers. One of the Germans looked in Giorgio's direction. After the colonel finished his discussion, he returned to the front of the room. He stopped short of the sergeant and addressed all of the soldiers.

"Gentleman of the Italian Royal Army, we have a problem here that needs to be addressed. We have some here who think what we're doing isn't the best course of action for this country. They also think that gathering other soldiers to join their cause is acceptable. This is in violation of our military code and will cease now. It is called treason, and it will not be tolerated. Those of you who are thinking of joining these groups, stop and think about what could happen to you and your families. Those of you who have already embarked on this dreadful course will be dealt with swiftly and harshly."

As the colonel prepared to leave the barracks, the two German officers scanned the faces of the Italian men. One of the officer's eyes locked onto Gino. His heart raced, and when the officer looked away he backpedaled toward the window. Giacomo grabbed his elbow and whispered, "Steady, my friend. They don't want us."

Two German soldiers entered the barracks and grabbed Giorgio's arms, escorting him away. Sergeant Sal waited for the Germans to clear out and then addressed the men. "Gentleman, we will fall out of the barracks and into ranks to watch the soldier in question have his trial for treason. Now fall out."

It only took about two minutes for everybody to gather their jackets and hats and get into ranks outside. Giorgio stood between two soldiers with his hands tied behind his back. Gino and Giacomo were in front because they were already dressed and came out before most of the other soldiers. The sergeant called the troops to attention. The colonel asked Giorgio a series of questions related to anti-Axis-power meetings being held off the compound. Giorgio acknowledged going to the meetings but said they were not anti-Axis meetings but rather discussions of how to improve the country in its current state of confusion. As Giorgio completed his statement, Colonel Specca pointed to a small building next to the barracks. German soldiers opened a door and out came a man and woman dressed in all black. Both looked as if they had been beaten. The German soldiers escorted them to Giorgio, who now looked more defiant than scared.

The Italian colonel asked the two witnesses if this was the soldier attending the rally. They pointed to Giorgio and nodded. The two were then whisked away and put back into the building.

The German officers approached the colonel, leaned in, whispered and then stepped back. Colonel Specca flashed the officers a look of disgust but complied with their orders.

"Private Giorgio Giovani, you have been found guilty of all crimes and will face a firing squad. May God have mercy on your soul."

The soldiers grabbed Giorgio and escorted him to a wall of the building where the couple had emerged earlier. There, a line of Italian and German soldiers waited with rifles in hand. Sergeant Sal blindfolded Giorgio and whispered something in his ear. He lit a cigarette and put it in Giorgio's mouth, then departed with head hanging low. Giorgio spat out the cigarette and yelled, "The hell with the Axis powers; support the Allies!"

The soldiers raised their rifles, took aim, and the colonel gave the gesture to end Giorgio's life.

At about 0700 the next morning, Gino and Giacomo were getting their jackets to head out for their work assignments when they noticed a crowd by the window near Sergeant Sal's room. They went to see what the fuss was all about. Gino was revolted but not surprised to see the man and woman who condemned Giorgio hanging from a tree by their necks with caps over the heads.

Giacomo pointed at a sign at the bottom of the tree. It read, *This couple was guilty of treason and sentenced to death by hanging.*

***

Gino immediately thought about his visits, albeit infrequent, to his hometown to see his wife. Security had tightened; the Germans continued to crack down on deserters. If caught, the

Germans would surely end his life and his wife's. Still, he missed his family desperately and couldn't fathom not seeing them again. He needed a new plan, and he would need Giacomo's help.

Chapter 13

GINO HAD NOT BEEN able to travel to Pordenone for quite some time. He stayed loosely in touch with his family by befriending civilians, usually older men or women, who traveled from Rome to Venice and to Pordenone and beyond the Italian borders. These travelers would take letters and bring back information from the workers' families on a regular basis. Of course, there was a fee or some sort of bartering. Gino learned that Catherina was expecting their second child, and Giacomo received a letter saying his family was safe and doing well. They were happy about their situations but needed to decide what to do if things went the wrong way in Rome.

As the summer weather improved, the amount of work for the soldiers in Rome increased. The winter had been colder than normal, compounding problems with the city's electrical grid. They were so busy that Gino had convinced Colonel Specca that he and Giacomo needed their own vehicle so they could work more efficiently. Hours wasted being transported with laborers could be spent repairing electrical lines, Gino argued.

The colonel, wanting to please the Germans, agreed and was able to find a Taunus sedan they converted into a work vehicle. They moved all their tools, cables, switch boxes, and about anything they needed into this sedan so they could get any job done. The only stipulation was the car had to be parked in front of the barracks each evening, with the only exception being if they were on an emergency job.

"What do you think the problem is, Giacomo?" asked Gino.

Giacomo inspected a fuse that wasn't working correctly. The fuse fed an apartment full of German soldiers.

"Well, the leads looked burnt, and it was most likely singed because these scums use too much electricity. We could tell them we can't fix it and move onto the other jobs."

"Isn't this the third time this week we've had to fix this problem?"

"No, I think it's the fourth."

They chuckled; they were making their visitors uncomfortable without getting into trouble. Giacomo pulled out the old fuse while Gino readied a modified used one for installation. Normally, they would replace the old fuse with a new one. But in this situation, they made a slight modification to the fuse. Nothing the ordinary eye would catch, but a trained electrician would notice the leads were set to fail earlier than normal. He snapped it into place and power returned to the apartment building.

Gino was in the driver's seat when Giacomo climbed in the passenger side. They'd modified the passenger seat due to his height, back problems and eyesight issues. Gino put the car into gear and headed toward their next job, which was about a kilometer away.

As they pulled out of the driveway, a German car pulled in behind them. Gino stopped the car, and Giacomo turned to see a German and an Italian officer in the car blocking them.

"What do they want from us?" remarked Gino. Both officers approached their makeshift work truck.

"Are you the electricians?" asked the Italian officer.

"Yes sir! What can we do for you?"

"You need to follow us. There has been an emergency and we need you to fix an electrical issue at one of our hotels."

"I am sorry, sir, but we have strict orders from our colonel not to go anywhere except for our work orders."

Giacomo held the paper showing their assignments for the day. The Italian officer raised his head over the car's roof and looked at the German officer, who was standing straight with his thumbs in his black belt looking at Giacomo. He was in no mood for belligerence and told the Italian officer so in German.

The German wore a black uniform with matching hat. Giacomo had his right hand on the door handle, and his left held a nine-inch assault knife hidden underneath the work-order paperwork. He wasn't going to let some Gestapo thug take his life without a fight. He was ready to make his move when the Italian made an offer.

"What if we gave you some money and cigarettes for your time?"

Giacomo's grip eased.

"We're listening to your offer. What's the job?" asked Gino.

"The Hotel Roma needs better electricity for its residents. We will give you a month's pay and a case of cigarettes."

Gino knew what hotel they were talking about and how important it was to the officers. It was their playhouse, complete with a bar, girls and gambling.

"How about a month's pay for each of us and two cases of cigarettes, and we will make the hotel our first priority every morning."

The Italian looked at Gino for a minute and walked over to his German companion to discuss their counteroffer. As the German left the passenger side of the car, Giacomo returned the assault knife to its resting place under the passenger seat. Gino waited for about ten minutes before he got out to see what was taking so long. The officers waved him over.

"We will give you the pay and cigarettes if you also make sure the officer barracks is checked every day as well," the Italian officer said.

The German carried two cases of cigarettes from their trunk to the electricians' car, and the Italian handed Gino a stack of money thick enough to be two months' pay.

"Now go fix the Hotel Roma and make sure the electricity stays on at the barracks."

Gino took the money and watched them get into their car and pull away. He counted the money, took half and handed Giacomo his cut.

"Thank you, sir! Shall we head toward the Hotel Roma to

make the necessary repairs?"

"Well, I think we should. Can I get one of those new cigarettes?"

"Not until the Germans get their power, mister," Giacomo said, chuckling with his partner.

***

Hotel Roma was outside of Rome's southern city limits and beyond the control of the Roman Catholics and local police. Everybody knew if the Germans wanted anything, they usually received it, and this playhouse was no exception. The hotel was a gesture from the Italian Fascists to make the Germans happy. The hotel had been a popular retreat for local politicians, military and business partners to meet and set rules. It was also the place for gambling, drinking and prostitution, for which it was now primarily used by the Germans.

It was built in 1930 with a grand entrance, spiral stairway leading to the bar, a complete kitchen, and more than fifty rooms, including three suites usually occupied by senior military officials. The building was off the main highway into southern Rome that connected most of Italy's major cities, including Naples. The exterior was white marble, and a grand stairway led to the entrance, which had two Norwegian oak doors that stretched over twenty feet high and were closed most of the time. Entrance into the hotel was made through an adjacent door. Most regulars used a side entrance, which was often crowded with patrons and military officers. Enlisted personnel were forbidden, except those who worked at the hotel.

"Wow, this is a nice hotel. Nothing like the ones we work on in Rome," said Gino as they pulled up. Giacomo nodded and guided his large frame out of the sedan. No cars were parked in front of the hotel, which meant they were in the wrong place. Gino started to say something to Giacomo, but it was too late; his friend was already climbing the stairs to those huge doors. He decided to follow. Giacomo was about to knock on the huge door when the smaller side door opened to reveal a doorman.

"This hotel is for military officers—not enlisted personnel. Have a nice day," said the doorman as he closed the door.

Giacomo looked at Gino with a huge smile and said, "Let's get out of here."

Gino walked past his friend to knock on the side door. The doorman opened the door, and before he could say anything Gino said, "We are here to work on the hotel."

The doorman responded, "What kind of work, and why aren't you using the side entrance like everyone else?"

"Well, that would explain why there aren't any cars in front. We're here to fix the electrical problems the hotel is currently having."

"Wait here; I'll be right back."

As they waited, a long black sedan pulled into the entrance and parked behind their work vehicle. An enlisted German chauffeur emerged and opened the back door of the sedan. Out came a senior German officer in all black. He wore a German pistol on his side, long black boots, and his uniform's creases were sharp enough to cut. An attractive young lady slid out of the back seat after the well-pressed officer.

Gino could tell she was a local girl and not a German. The officer held out his right arm and the pretty lady slid her left into the crook as they walked up the stairs. Gino and Giacomo saluted as they stepped by. As Gino stood motionless with his right arm extended, the side door opened. The doorman gave the Italians a dirty look and held the door open for the newly arrived couple.

"Good afternoon, Colonel. Glad to see you again. I hope you enjoy your stay. Your suite is ready. We have already checked you in and I will make sure your bags are taken to your suite," said the doorman.

The colonel tipped the doorman and led his lady friend into the hotel without a word.

"Hurry up and give me a hand with their bags. I will show you where to park your truck and the electrical problems."

Giacomo and doorman retrieved the colonel's bags while Gino moved their truck to the side of the hotel. Gino was standing at the bar sipping a beer when Giacomo came through the main lobby.

"How did you get a beer?"

"I asked the bartender for one and he gave me one. I figure I had nothing to lose but a beer."

They laughed as Giacomo held up his hand for a beer as well. They stood inconspicuously by the bar and looked around at the ornate scene.

"As far as I can tell, there don't seem to be any electrical problems here. I walked through most of the lobby and some of the other areas of the hotel, all of which had electricity working just fine," said Giacomo.

A loud sound came from a distance—a train headed into Rome from Naples. As the train passed, the lights in bar went out and so did half the lobby lights.

"Well, that answers a lot of questions," remarked Giacomo.

Once the train passed, all the lights came back on. They finished their beers, tipped the bartender, and walked the grounds to find where the electrical connections came into the hotel. They spotted wires coming from a huge distribution panel by the railroad tracks.

"Well, I guess we should go over there and see what's happening," remarked Gino.

They walked across a field of tall grass to the railroad tracks about 400 meters from the hotel and crossed the tracks to where the wires came down the pole and into the panel.

"This must be the main panel for this whole area. There must be a loose wire or connection somewhere," remarked Gino.

They looked up and down the panel, careful not to touch anything for fear of being shocked.

"There is the main switch, but it has a lock on it. I wonder who has the key?" asked Gino.

"I don't know, but it has a German sign on it. Let's go back to the truck and get our tools so we can fix this problem and go back to Rome."

"You go ahead and get the tools. I'm going to see if I can find the problem."

About fifteen minutes later, Giacomo returned with tools, but Gino was nowhere to be found. He called for his friend instead of walking to look for him. Giacomo's back was bothering him, and so was his good eye.

"Gino, where are you?"

"Over here, and I found the problem, but I don't think it's a problem. More of a situation."

Giacomo walked over.

"Look at this switch someone put here. If you flip the switch, all the electricity will go out at the hotel. But it's broken, so that's why the vibration of the train shorts it and only some of the lights go out. This switch was spliced in without ever taking the lock off the main panel. Look at where it's tied into the line. They covered it with rocks, but it looks like the big tree branch over there may have hit this switch when it fell, or something else happened to cause this switch to go bad."

"I'll bet the only reason this is here is so that someone can turn the lights off at the hotel and enter at night to kidnap or kill people," the always suspicious Giacomo said.

"I was thinking the same thing. Do we repair the switch or remove it?" responded Gino.

Giacomo retrieved a new switch connector and some jumper wire from the toolbox. In five minutes, he had it fixed without any assistance from Gino.

"I guess we should bury the switch, go back to the hotel and wait for a train to come by to see if we fixed the problem. We should do this in the bar to make sure the lights are okay."

They buried the device and packed up the tools.

As they entered the bar, they saw four German officers drinking beer and the bartender cleaning glasses. They walked to the bar and ordered two beers. As they waited for their beers, the doorman walked in and headed for them.

"What are you two doing in the bar? I told you; no enlisted allowed in here. Why are you not working on the electrical problem?"

"We are working, and we're having a beer while waiting to see if our repair works," replied Giacomo. The bartender placed two beers in front of them.

"Waiting for what?"

"We are waiting for a train," they answered, picking up their beers and taking a sip.

"Why are you waiting for a train in the bar where you're not supposed to be in the first place?"

"We think we fixed the problem, so we need to make sure the lights don't go out when a train goes by the hotel. The train vibration may be causing the lights to go out. We have to wait and see, so we figured we might as well have a beer while waiting. Please let us do our jobs."

Gino saw the Germans listening to their conversation. The doorman was agitated and about to call hotel security when everyone in the bar stood and saluted at the same time. The German colonel entered with his lady in tow. They were going to have a few cocktails before dinner.

"Let them stay and drink a beer. I am tired of my lights going off and on all the time," said the colonel. "Everyone go back to your drinks and don't mind us. We will be sitting in back waiting to be served."

Giacomo relaxed as the colonel passed him and gave the doorman a get-lost gesture with his right hand. The doorman turned and left the bar. Gino and his friend sat and drank their beers, wondering how long until the next train passed. Gino couldn't help but notice the bartender looking at them as if he were hiding something or keeping a secret. The bartender poured them two more beers.

"These beers are on me, guys. I hate the doorman, and to see him get put in his place makes for the best day ever."

Giacomo and Gino smiled and raised their beers in a toast.

"Do you know when the next train will come by the hotel?" asked Gino.

The bartender looked at his watch. "In fifteen minutes."

"Well, we have time for one more after this one, and then we need to head back to Rome."

The bar was getting more patrons and the noise level picked up. They were on their third beer when they heard the familiar sound of a distant train approaching. As the train got closer, Gino turned around to see everyone at the bar staring at him and Giacomo. News traveled quickly; everyone wanted to know if these two electricians from Rome fixed their problem. The train came and passed without a light even flickering. Everyone in the bar cheered and clapped; even the bartender smiled.

"Well done, gentlemen. Those beers are on me," said the colonel as he left with his lady friend smiling at the electricians. The bartender nodded and extended his hand to thank them for their excellent work.

"My name is Enrico, and thank you for all your help,"

remarked their new bartender friend. Gino felt something in his hand after the bartender shook it. He quickly put whatever it was in his right pocket. It might be money.

On the drive back to Rome, Gino stopped the car and reached into his pocket to pull out what was handed to him. It was a folded sheet of paper.

"What is it?" asked Giacomo.

"The bartender gave it to me when he shook our hands."

"Well, what does it say?"

Gino opened the note and read it out loud.

"All Italian soldiers' lives are in danger. It is only a matter of time before you are killed, sent to the front, or imprisoned. Come see me if you want to live."

"There is some truth to this letter, Gino. Maybe we should go back tomorrow and see what he has to offer us. It is only an amount of time before we get sent to the front and die, while those German scum get to stay alive drinking our wine, taking our women, and staying in our hotels."

Gino knew his partner was right; there weren't too many Italian soldiers left in Rome.

"It's only a matter of time before we get the short end of the stick. I guess we'll go back to the hotel tomorrow and see what he has to offer us," answered Gino.

Chapter 14

IN THE SUMMER OF 1942, just about all the regular Italian forces in Rome were gone. The Germans ran the city with only a few senior Italian officers. There were a few essential Italian soldiers as well—mostly men like Gino and Giacomo spared from the battlefront to make sure the city ran normally. For the most part, Rome was a Nazi playground.

Gino and Giacomo worked directly for the Germans. Only one senior Italian officer, Colonel Specca, remained in charge of their unit, and he was mostly a figurehead. There were benefits for working directly for the Germans, and the two men used it to their advantage. As long as electricity was running fine in their buildings and hotels, the Germans left the electricians alone.

All the other wounded Italian soldiers who had shared the barracks with them were long gone. Gino and Giacomo had the run of the place. Only the severely wounded Italians were spared the long journey to the Eastern Front. Some were lucky enough to be sent back home because the Italian army and Germans had no use for them and didn't want the expense of caring for them. They were more of a burden than an asset to Mussolini's conquering dreams.

***

"We need to get going, Gino. We have a lot of territory to cover today, and the Germans want to make sure they're getting their electricity. Plus, we need to stop by the German compound and get our new assignments. Hopefully they haven't asked us to join the fight in the Eastern Front," Giacomo said as he dressed for the day's events.

Gino noticed his friend was moving better than he did when they first met, but Gino didn't say anything to the lumbering oaf. Giacomo's vision was still a factor. Gino grew tired of driving every day. He couldn't count how many times Giacomo had fallen asleep in the car as they moved around the city fixing just about any problem that needed their attention. They were even tasked with work unrelated to electricity, but they didn't care as long as they were not on the front fighting.

"You know, I haven't been back since my wife had the baby. I wonder if the Germans would let me go on leave to see them?" asked Gino.

Giacomo tied his boots, raised his head and replied, "I am sure they'll let you go up north while the problems of Rome are on hold. No, they would undoubtedly send us to the front before allowing us any leave. We have discussed this many times in past. It's best to see what happens in the near future before we try to get back home. Now get dressed. I am hungry and want to eat before we head to the compound."

It was still cold in the mornings, but the afternoons were pleasant enough to leave their jackets in the sedan as they went from job to job.

Just before the German compound, Gino stopped the car in front of their favorite pastry store—the German Army Galley, which opened around the same time as the Germans took over the city. It wasn't the best food in the city, but it was free to the military. The morning meals were usually good, and whatever they were serving was fresh.

Giacomo got out of the sedan and made his way into the small galley. As he exited their work vehicle, Gino noticed a black German sedan pulling into the compound just ahead of them. This was a normal occurrence in this area, so it didn't faze him. He looked at the galley and for the first time noticed it must have been an Italian bakery at one time. The new sign was painted over an older one. The building looked like it was painted a faded white, but it was hard to tell since there were areas the plaster had fallen off during previous winters. He smiled knowing they perhaps had someone open the galley for their troops in Rome, but he didn't care because the food was free. Something caught Gino's eye—something bright. He glanced back at the bright object and noticed the cargo in their back seat wasn't covered up. Gino jumped over the front seats and moved their gear and tools to cover their illegal cargo—small arms and ammunition.

Most of the items were only theirs for a short time, but if they were searched, it would be a problem. They could say that they found it while working in one of the German buildings and were returning it to the German compound. More likely, they would face a firing squad.

Gino and Giacomo were smuggling weapons and other illegal items for the bartender Enrico. It was part of an agreement they came up with a couple of months ago, after he gave Gino the letter at the bar. The electricians didn't want to join a rebellion against the Germans for fear of being killed, but they devised a plan that would benefit both parties.

***

When Giacomo exited the bakery, his partner was standing outside the car.

"Hey, we need to do a better job hiding this cargo or we're going to be put in front of a firing squad."

He smiled at Gino as he got into the front seat. "If you yell a little louder, maybe the Germans will hear you."

The smell of the pastries made him hungry, so Gino jumped into the driver's seat ready to eat. The same black sedan they saw earlier left the compound, but without passengers.

"I wonder who was dropped off?" remarked Giacomo with a mouth full of breakfast delight.

After they had a quick breakfast of pastries and coffee, Gino put the car in gear and pulled into the compound in their usual spot left of the office building. Gino always backed the car in so the trunk faced the wall. Giacomo got out of the sedan, but instead of heading toward the office building he opened the trunk.

Why would he open the trunk in the compound? thought Gino.

The Germans never checked the sedan while they were at the compound, but you could never be too careful. Before Gino could get out to see what Giacomo was doing, the trunk closed. In Giacomo's hands were cigarettes and candy, gifts for Sergeant Lucciano and Gilda Deluca, the colonel's secretary. They both took care of them, so in return the electricians gave them gifts.

Sergeant Lucciano was strictly an administrative soldier with no battlefield experience. He was never sent to the front line during his five years in the military. Everything he did was to ensure that this streak was kept intact.

Gilda Deluca's skills as a secretary were limited to typing, phone calls and appointments. She had other skills that were needed by the resistance.

***

After their meeting with Enrico, they devised a plan to smuggle items for the rebellion. Since the hotel was their first stop every morning as required by the Germans, they parked their sedan near the bar with their trunk facing the wooded area in the back. They would take out their toolboxes but leave the trunk open as they entered the hotel. The hotel was now asking them to fix not only electrical problems but also plumbing and just about anything else that needed attention. If Enrico's men put anything in the trunk, all Gino and Giacomo had to do was transport the goods to the other side of the city to avoid German checkpoints at the main train station and roads leading into Rome.

When they finished their daily work at the hotel, they loaded their tools in the open trunk and left. They would check their cargo and take what they needed as payment for their service to the rebellion, but for the most part they delivered the goods untouched.

The drop-off was at a factory north of the city. Using the same routine they used at the bar, the trunk was left open facing a wooded area. When they finished their work in the factory, their sedan was usually a little lighter. They didn't care who took the goods. This sometimes worked in the reverse; they would pick up goods from the factory and deliver them to the hotel. They also acquired quite a few goods they hoarded for themselves—cigarettes, food rations, clothes, and blankets—and a few infantry service rifles, Beretta handguns, and enough ammunition to get them out of Rome if they needed to escape. The barracks floorboards provided the best hiding places, but they had trouble stockpiling all of their goods. When they had a chance, they smuggled supplies to their families through their contact at the factory, a salesman that frequently traveled to northern Italy.

Giacomo would always go into the office building because the Germans never bothered him due to his size and disfigured face. They thought him harmless and feeble. Gino had a cigarette while he waited for his coworker to come back. As he finished his first draw, he noticed a German officer in all black with a red armband standing near the corridor used by his workmate moments ago. The officer looked like he was waiting for someone. Gino looked away. The officer looked familiar, but Gino couldn't place him. After another draw off the cigarette, he noticed the officer walking toward him. Gino stood at attention.

"What's in the sedan, Private?" asked the German as he got closer.

"We're the city electricians working for your colonel to keep the lights on in every building. We also do plumbing, woodwork and anything else the colonel wants done. The sedan is how we get the tools and gear to the jobsite. Would you like a cigarette, sir?"

He handed a cigarette to the officer. The officer took the cigarette and let Gino light it for him.

"I don't work for your colonel. I am here to make sure everything is running smoothly," replied the officer, looking for any signs of guilt in Gino's eyes. "I've seen you before. Did you work in the ghetto some time ago?"

Gino recognized the man now; he was one of the officers who had Giacomo beaten in the ditch.

***

As Giacomo made his way to the office to receive their marching orders, he heard someone yelling at their top of their lungs. Most folks were moving away from the entrance of the office, but he was unfazed. As he turned into the office, he saw a German colonel scolding Colonel Specca. The German colonel was the one at the hotel the first time Giacomo and Gino visited months ago; he was a regular, always with different women in tow when he visited. Giacomo approached the task desk where Sergeant Lucciano would hand him their orders. The sergeant stood at attention without moving a muscle. Giacomo approached the desk with a crisp march and stood at attention like everyone else in the office.

As the colonel exited the back office he yelled, "When you find out who knows what's going on in Rome, give me a call!"

When the colonel left the office, everyone went back to work, including Sergeant Lucciano. Giacomo smiled at the sergeant and asked, "What do you have for us today?"

"Here are your work orders. The colonel does that about once a week and leaves as though he's some type of Officer God. It gets old, if you know what I mean," commented the senior enlisted. Giacomo took the work orders without losing his smile and relaxed.

"He's undoubtedly feeling the heat from his superiors, which means he's decided to inflict his pain on everyone else. Are there going to be any surprise visitors or meetings we need to know about, Sergeant?" asked Giacomo, handing him the daily bribe of cigarettes.

The cigarettes ensured the electricians were updated on just about everything that could get them in trouble. The sergeant also shared information on where the Germans were doing random road checks or building inspections.

Lucciano looked around before he grabbed the cigarettes from his visitor. "There is nothing planned for today."

Giacomo winked at the sergeant before he turned to leave. He stopped at Gilda's desk and gave her his best smile before handing her the candy she liked so much. She reddened and slid the delights in her snack drawer.

Giacomo was making his way out to the sedan when he saw the Gestapo officer talking to Gino. He needed to act quickly because he knew they would eventually find something wrong to harass the Italian about and justify their existence. Giacomo stopped a German soldier standing by the door smoking a cigarette.

"Excuse me, buddy, but who is the Gestapo officer over there?"

The soldier looked over in Gino's direction. "Major Schmidt. Gestapo."

Giacomo handed the soldier a pack of cigarettes and thanked him as he went to Gino and Major Schmidt.

"Excuse me, sir, is your name Major Schmidt?" asked Giacomo as he closed the distance.

Major Schmidt turned around and looked at the giant Italian with shock and suspicion.

"Who wants to know?"

"Sir, I am a messenger, but the German colonel was yelling at Colonel Specca and asking for you to call him."

Schmidt had heard the yelling. He finished his cigarette and walked off. Giacomo looked at Gino and said, "Let's get out of here before he comes back."

"You could have not been timelier," Gino said as he pulled away. "He was about to inspect the sedan. What did the colonel want with him?"

"The colonel was yelling at Specca and said if he finds the person who knows what's going on here, he wanted them to call him. I took that to mean he wanted the major to call him because the Gestapo always knows what's going on in the city."

They laughed nervously and headed to the hotel for a scheduled stop and unload.

"We need to be more careful and make sure we don't have anything in the sedan when we go to the compound in the mornings," Giacomo said, still laughing. "We'll face a firing squad of our own weapons."

Chapter 15

GILDA DELUCA WAS BUSY typing the latest memorandum for Colonel Specca—an article for the local newspaper outlining how well the Fascist movement was doing abroad. As she typed, a dark object caught her attention. She looked to see her office companion standing at attention and the ever-present Nazi major heading toward the colonel's office and entering without knocking.

"What do you need from me now, Colonel Specca?" asked the major.

The Italian colonel lowered the newspaper he was reading.

"Major Schmidt, I want nothing from you. Why are you here?" replied the colonel.

The colonel was the only Italian military person in Rome who didn't have to stand at attention when the major came into a room because he outranked him.

"I was told by one of your enlisted personnel you were looking for me."

The colonel stood to meet the major's eyes and responded, "I did not ask for the Gestapo, and since when do you listen to junior people, anyway?"

Schmidt was getting angry but knew the colonel was correct. As he was getting ready to leave, he saw Gino and Giacomo's sedan speed away through the colonel's window. The major's stern look turned to a smile when he realized the large Italian soldier had tricked him.

Clever, thought the major. *But let's see who gets the last laugh.*

The major stood in the corridor, cooling down before going to meet with his supervisor, the German colonel. As he walked, he studied the building's construction. *Beautiful but impractical and gaudy. Just like the Italians,* he thought. The massive corridor was an open breezeway, which made it pleasant in the summer and spring months, but during the winter months the wind was sure to catch your attention. Arched Roman columns supported the roof.

The German colonel was settling in for the day's events when Major Schmidt entered his secretary's office.

"Have the major come into my office," yelled the colonel. Major Schmidt did not even stop to acknowledge the secretary as he entered his immediate supervisor's inner office.

"Shut the door, Major."

The major took his usual seat in front of the colonel's desk.

"Major Schmidt, it looks like we're going to have some visitors in the upcoming week. Does the Gestapo know of any reason why my superiors are coming here?"

"Herr Colonel, I don't know why. My reports have all been normal, with the exception of the isolated treason cases."

"See if you can make some phone calls to dig into this manner. The more we know about this visit, the better we can prepare and avoid any unnecessary transfers. I'm certainly not interested in going to the front lines, are you?"

In truth, Major Schmidt would much rather be leading tanks into battle than shuffling paperwork and dealing with shifty Italians and cowardly bureaucrats in Rome.

Schmidt acknowledged the order but had no intention of making the calls. He didn't work for the colonel. He was the Gestapo and answered to a higher authority than the common army colonel. Perhaps they were coming to reassign him to lead a tank command. A lieutenant could do Schmidt's job in Rome with one eye shut. But few could marshal tanks like the great Major Schmidt. They were going to need all of their best

Germans for the next invasion.

"Is there anything else you would like to discuss, Herr Major? How is the way station in the ghetto coming along?"

The major couldn't believe he was asking this question. It had been in use for three months.

"The station is complete. We already processed people back to the homeland weeks ago."

"Good. I need to go down there and see this way station in operation. When are you going there next?"

"Tomorrow morning after our meeting."

The German colonel thought about it for a minute and checked his schedule.

"Sounds good. Tomorrow it is, and don't tell anybody I'm coming. We want this to be a surprise."

The major nodded, stood and left the colonel's office. Now he wanted to find the crafty Italian who tricked him. Most of the Italian enlisted were housed in German-controlled compounds, so they shouldn't be too hard to find. There were only a few still operating, as most Italian soldiers were deployed to battlefronts.

***

Lieutenant Muller was pulling into the compound and he could see the ever-present major standing in the corridor looking at the roof. He slowed the sedan as the major lowered his head from looking into the sky. After he stopped the sedan, the lieutenant quickly exited the vehicle to open the door for his immediate supervisor and mentor. Major Schmidt was already standing waiting for the lieutenant to open the door as he approached him. The lieutenant reached for the door handle when the major spoke. "Where do those Italian military electricians live?" asked Major Schmidt.

"Which electricians are you talking about, Herr Major?"

"The ones that Sergeant Braun was supposed to make an example of to make sure we had the Italians' attention. They also did all the work at the way station and the ghetto."

"I don't know, Herr Major, but I will find out for you as soon as I take you to your office."

The major glanced around the compound to see who was looking in his direction. There was no one. He was sure the joke pulled on him was an isolated one. The only ones that knew of his embarrassment were the privates and their colonel. The Hero of Hannut would have his revenge.

"Let's go by the ghetto before you take me to the office," ordered the major.

The lieutenant put the car in gear before heading to the ghetto.

"Lieutenant, I want you to make sure everything is in order at the way station for tomorrow morning. Our colonel will be stopping by for a surprise visit with me after our morning meeting. Let no one know he is coming, and you don't know as well."

"Yes, Herr Major."

***

After leaving Major Schmidt, the junior officer set out to find the two electricians, who were obviously in some kind of danger. He had seen the electricians at some point mustering with the other soldiers near the barracks west of the city. That was a long time ago, and most of the soldiers were long gone by now. No one could forget the large, one-eyed Italian soldier, so getting the location of these soldiers wouldn't be hard. The lieutenant had to make sure his information was accurate before telling the major. Those who gave the major wrong information usually paid the price.

As the compound came into the view, the lieutenant slowed the sedan to turn into the large parking area. The lot was empty this afternoon, with the exception of an old working truck that had seen better days. The lieutenant spotted Sergeant Lucciano having lunch just outside the office building.

"Where is the compound commanding officer?" the lieutenant asked.

"Herr Colonel Specca has gone to lunch."

"No matter. I am not here for the colonel. Perhaps you can help me. I need to talk to you about some of your Italian workers."

"What can I help you with?"

"I am looking for the two electricians that come here every morning for their work assignments. Where do they live?"

The sergeant looked confused. "They stay at the barracks

across from the main train station. That is where they've always stayed. Do I need to move them somewhere else?"

"No, you don't have to move them," answered the German officer as he turned to head back to his car.

"That's good because I need to get ahold of them and let them know their new work truck is here. Their old one was a converted sedan. They're so busy making repairs around the city we decided to get them a replacement before they break down somewhere."

The lieutenant stopped in his tracks. He turned back to Lucciano, holding out his hand.

"Let me deliver the new truck to them," he said coyly.

The sergeant went back into the office, grabbed some paperwork and came back into the compound yard.

"You need to sign this paperwork, Lieutenant."

After the lieutenant signed, the sergeant said, "The truck is yours."

***

Major Schmidt returned to his office to prepare for the visit and catch up on his paperwork. He sat at his desk thinking about his beautiful Hilda, the beautiful nurse who made him feel alive again. He looked forward to her visit later in the year.

Getting through all the paperwork was mundane. The major wondered if he would ever return to the tank battles that made him a hero not too long ago. Staying in this city was killing him. Fighting the enemy with Panzer tanks was his destiny. The newer version of the Panzer was coming out, and for the first time since the Panzer was developed for battle, he was going to miss the design and testing phases. Just thinking about it made his head pound.

How could they not want input from the Hero of Hannut? he thought as he reached into his desk for pills to relieve his headache. Marta Columbo walked into his office.

"Lieutenant Muller is on the line for you, Herr Major." The major waved at her to patch the call into him as he swallowed his relief with a sip of water. He grabbed his phone.

"Herr Major, I have found the electricians. They still live in the barracks near the main train station. The colonel ordered them a new work truck, which I signed for and will be delivering to them."

"Excellent work, Lieutenant. Come to my office and we'll deliver the truck together and see if these jokers have anything that will hold them accountable for their insubordinate actions this morning."

"I am on my way, Major."

The lieutenant immediately headed out to the major's office. *I wonder what those poor electricians did to the major,* he thought.

Chapter 16

GINO PULLED INTO THE hotel in the same manner as he had done for the past few months. This time he didn't leave the trunk open for fear someone was watching. Giacomo stayed in the sedan to make sure all was clear before they proceeded with the drop. As Gino walked into the bar, the first thing he noticed was the bartender cleaning glasses with a towel. The bartender looked up and gestured toward the back of the bar, to the storage room. Gino usually walked into the front lobby for work, but this morning he headed into the bar's storage room from the back way so as not to be seen.

As he entered the room, Enrico asked, "What happened at the compound this morning?"

Gino looked confused. "What are you talking about? What problem?"

"The incident with the Gestapo major. Apparently, he's upset about something and has been inquiring about you and Giacomo."

"How do you know about that?

"We have people all over the city and word travels fast."

"Let me tell you something, if you are going to spy on us, we're going to stop doing business with you. Do you understand me? We are putting our lives in jeopardy for you, and the more people who know what we're doing, the more likely we could get caught. We have some new rules we're going by or we stop this today." Gino waved his finger in Enrico's face and finished with, "Do you understand me!"

The bartender stepped back and realized the Italian soldier had the upper hand, and he didn't want to make him angrier.

"Mr. Cartelli, I apologize for my outburst, but we wanted to make sure you were alright this morning. The eyes are on the Germans and not you. We don't want to cause you harm in any way. Your partner and you are doing us a great service, which is helping us shape the new Europe for a better future for all. What are the new rules to make you feel safer? I was just trying to give you a warning."

The war had been going poorly for the Italians, and the Germans continued to crack down, sensing an uprising. They were becoming more diligent and unforgiving of anyone who undermined the cause. Suddenly, Gino's confidence waned and he felt endangered. He and Giacomo might have to make a move if detected. The mishap with the Gestapo major certainly didn't help matters.

"In the past we would leave the trunk open so your folks could load their equipment for transport; we need to alter the plan a bit. If the trunk is closed, that will be our sign we feel unsafe or we need to go someplace where the car will be inspected, so we can't have any of your goods in the back. The second change will be that we have to deliver the equipment on the same day; there will be no overnight storage."

Enrico nodded. "That's no problem. We can adjust to those changes. Can you guys get a bigger truck or some type of trailer so we can move more items?"

Gino said, "Since we have been tasked to do more than electrical work in the past couple of months, we've asked for a new service truck, but so far nothing from our Italian or German colonels. Hell, I don't know who's in charge anymore."

"Well, let's have a drink to celebrate our new agreement, Mr. Cartelli."

"That sounds great. Let me get my partner and open the trunk for your delivery today."

***

As they drove back to the barracks, they were tired and a bit worried. The work was intensifying as well as the scrutiny. They finished another twelve-hour day without any breaks, and there was more to do tomorrow. As Gino pulled off the main highway, he felt like something was wrong. He stopped before they got to the barracks.

"What are you doing? Let's go. I'm hungry," remarked Giacomo.

"I'm worried about us being watched; and I'm worried about that German major we ran from. Do we have anything in the truck that could get us in trouble?"

"I don't think so—just my pistol. But let's check one more time. You never know who's going to be at the barracks."

They opened the trunk to see if anything could get them in trouble. They moved some tools, buckets and paint, and something caught Gino's eye. Tucked into the corner were two boxes of rifle ammunition.

"How did we miss those boxes?"

"I don't know, but let's take a look at the whole sedan to make sure there's nothing that can tie us to them."

They hid the ammunition in the nearest bush and off they went back to their sleeping quarters. As they closed in on the barracks, they noticed a small troop transporter in front of the barracks. Their first thought was they had company in the barracks. They only saw the troop transports when soldiers were being moved from one place to another. There was an Opel Blitz in front of the barracks as well.

It's seen better days, but it's still in good shape, thought Gino as he exited the work sedan to clean up before dinner.

They entered the barracks to see three people sitting in the makeshift lounge. Two of them were regular German soldiers, and the other was Major Schmidt.

"Glad to see you privates again. I hope you don't mind us sitting in your lounge," remarked the major. "You see, I received a call this afternoon that the lieutenant was bringing your new work truck, I decided to come along and join the fun since we had such a good time this morning." The major glared at Giacomo.

"You know what was funny about this morning? Colonel Specca had no idea what I was talking about when I went to see him. You told me the colonel wanted to see me, did you not, Private?"

The major rose and approached Giacomo, who had about fifty pounds of muscle on the German. "As it turns out, the colonel didn't want to see me at all. Now, why, I wonder, would a lowly Italian private make up such a lie to a Gestapo major?"

Both of the privates stood at attention. The one-eyed giant looked straight into the major's eyes without blinking and replied, "I apologize, sir, but I was in Colonel Specca's office when I heard the German colonel yell that he wanted the person who knew what was going on in Rome to report to him. I saw you standing next to Private Cartelli and thought a Gestapo major was the man to provide such a report to Colonel Specca and the German colonel. I apologize if I was wrong, Herr Major."

Major Schmidt looked at Giacomo for about a minute to see if he showed any signs of fear. If this were a lie, it was certainly bold and reckless, especially from a lowly Italian private.

"Well, I guess I can see how you could come up with that conclusion. But, Private, be warned. You have no business eavesdropping on discussions between officers. Doing so can be perilous, if you understand my meaning."

"Yes sir. Forgive me, sir. I will stick to only my business in the future."

"Okay then. You're lucky I'm in a good mood, and you're lucky your services are needed. To that end, I have a new work vehicle here for you. Go ahead and move all that equipment from your old car to the Opel. I've brought some reinforcements to help you move the equipment. Shall we go outside, privates?"

The major opened the door and both privates followed him. The two other soldiers were right behind them with their guns at the ready. As they filed outside, the lieutenant and at least five other soldiers stood where there were none earlier.

"Gentlemen, please assist our electricians in moving their gear from the small vehicle to the larger one," the major ordered the five soldiers standing at attention.

When Giacomo moved toward the old sedan to unload it, the major quickly put up his hand, signaling the German soldiers to aim their guns. Giacomo froze.

"Private, stand where you are for right now and don't move," ordered the major.

"Sir, I just want to get some personal items from the front seat before they get lost or stolen."

Schmidt summoned Lieutenant Muller.

"Show my junior officer what you want to get out of the car, Private."

Giacomo went to the passenger seat with Lieutenant Muller watching him like a hawk. Gino was about to make a run for it, thinking Giacomo had had enough and was going to pull a revolver hidden in the cab and start shooting, but Giacomo emerged carrying a wooden box Gino knew was full of letters and personal items. He breathed again as his partner rejoined him.

"Private, open the box and show my junior officer what's inside so we can move onto other important tasks at hand."

He opened the box, and the lieutenant moved the letters around with the barrel of his pistol. Seeing nothing suspicious, he signaled to the major that all was clear. Muller moved to the work sedan, which was already being unloaded by the soldiers, to look for any type of contraband. After the sedan was empty, the German soldiers looked under the car and in the engine compartment and every other space and cavity.

The search took almost a half hour, and once completed the major said something to the junior officer. Lieutenant Muller put his pistol away and ran behind the barracks. The major waited with his hands behind his back. Seconds later, a car rounded the corner and stopped in front of the major, who didn't move until a soldier opened the door for him. When the soldier shut the door, Lieutenant Muller put the car in gear and headed for the main highway. The other soldiers dispersed without a word. Neither private moved until all the Germans were out of sight.

"Well, that was fun," said Giacomo.

Gino was shaking.

"It was a good call checking the car one more time before we got here. Those boxes of ammunition would have been hard to explain to the major," Giacomo said, still holding the wooden box. He also held a pistol.

"Where did you get that gun?" asked Gino.

"It was in the bottom of the box. I took it out when everyone was watching the sedan being unloaded. I carved an opening on the bottom to hold my pens and other items, but a pistol fits nicely in there. I needed to retrieve the box before the soldiers found the gun; you know Italian privates are not allowed to have pistols."

Gino was speechless. His partner had a gun at the ready with Germans surrounding them.

"Giacomo, you're either crazy or suicidal."

"No, I'm mostly hungry. Let's go eat."

Chapter 17

MAJOR SCHMIDT HATED HIS new office down the corridor from Colonel Specca's. Schmidt's boss, the German colonel, was shipped to Russia to plan an upcoming invasion. That left Major Schmidt the highest-ranking German officer in the city. Although the Italian colonel still outranked the major, Schmidt's new position gave him more authority, which in turn made the colonel treat Schmidt with deference. The two men now met daily to ensure Schmidt was in the loop on all activities in Rome and Vatican City.

Major Schmidt was at his desk enjoying one of the few times when there wasn't much to do. He looked out his window and wished he were viewing the battlefield through field glasses instead. He sighed, knowing his days of commanding tanks were over. He had hoped that the recent visit to Rome by German officers would bring him better news. But it was news that his boss, the German colonel, was going to battle—not the once famous tank commander. Schmidt reached for his pills to find relief for his pounding head caused by the church bells' constant ringing. His door suddenly erupted with the familiar knocking of Marta Columbo, who had moved to his new office.

"Major, you have a call from up north."

"Who is it?"

"Major Klein from the Northern Italy Command."

"Good afternoon, Major Schmidt. This is Major Klein. I received a phone call from one of my Italian supporters from the Azzano-Decimo area. They caught a smuggler last week."

"What does that have to do with me?"

"After he was questioned, the man said there is a vast network of locals involved throughout Rome."

Schmidt sat up and grabbed a pen and paper to take notes.

"What was he smuggling?"

"Looks like he was smuggling mostly food, clothing items and blankets, which is nothing to worry about. But he was caught with some small-arm ammunition, too."

"Did he have any guns? And do you have names of the people? "

"No, he didn't have any guns when he was stopped, but he admitted later that he had smuggled weapons and ammunition in the past. The man, shall we say, perished before we got names from him. The only thing he told us was there were two farmers on a horse and cart he delivered to most of the time."

"Why are you bothering me about this small-time smuggler? I have bigger issues to deal with," replied Schmidt, getting ready to hang up.

"I understand, but there was some other information he told us that would be of use to you. The smuggler said he heard about two Italian soldiers in Rome who were smuggling bigger items for the resistance. The men work out of a truck full of tools. They are repairmen of some sort. He said they meet at a factory outside of Rome."

Schmidt immediately knew this could only be the two electricians he had issues with, but he could not do anything to them unless he caught them red-handed. They were the only military electricians in the city and he needed them.

"That is good information. Thank you for the phone call, Major. I will be in touch." Schmidt hung up with a huge smile.

***

Giacomo left the barracks to retrieve food and the work orders for today, and Gino decided to stay in the barracks and sleep in since it was still cold outside.

Since the incident with Major Schmidt, Gino and Giacomo had been cautious with their compound visits. They kept their work truck parked outside the compound and were more discreet with their visits and bribes to other Italian soldiers for information about German activities in the city.

Sergeant Lucciano loved his free cigarettes. If there were any issues, he placed a newspaper near the outer window of his office. This told Gino and Giacomo to stay away and call in for their work orders or come back at a later time. The chocolate-loving Gilda was also in on the messaging.

Gino sat in the empty barracks reading. The newspaper had the latest information about the horrible losses the Italians suffered in Russia. This wasn't good for Mussolini and the other Fascist leaders. The newspaper reported the Italian 8th Army had been just about annihilated—more than 20,000 soldiers killed and 64,000 taken prisoners. Only 45,000 soldiers returned to Italy. Those who made it back were starving, weak and bloodied. Most Italians were asking for Mussolini and the army generals to resign or be jailed for their decisions to invade Russia. Gino knew firsthand what the soldiers were going through based on his own experience in Ethiopia. He felt fortunate not to have been sent to the bitterly cold Russian front.

Gino realized Giacomo had been gone longer than normal. As he put the paper down, he heard vehicles pulling in front of the barracks. He made his way to the door to see who was visiting them.

Major Schmidt stepped from his sedan and seconds later the barracks door opened. German soldiers stormed in.

"What the hell do you think you're doing?" yelled Gino as the soldiers pushed him into the far corner of the room.

"Shut up, Private, and put your hands above your head," yelled Sergeant Braun, the same sergeant who beat Giacomo at the gravel pit.

"Where is the other one?" barked the major.

"He went to get our work orders. I'm surprised he's not with you. He went to your office building," Gino said sarcastically.

Braun gestured to one of the soldiers restraining Gino against the wall and the soldier rammed Gino in the stomach with the butt of his rifle. Gino collapsed, gasping.

"Where are you hiding all the items you're smuggling?" the sergeant yelled as he leaned over Gino.

Gino was still doubled over in pain and couldn't speak.

"If I have to ask you again, you're going to wish you never woke up this morning."

Gino put up his right hand and raised his index finger to signal he needed a minute to recover. Braun came down with a right hook that caught his chin. Gino's head hit the floor. As the sergeant prepared to strike again, the major stepped in.

"Let him recover or we will never find the items. Search the other rooms," Schmidt ordered the two soldiers holding Gino.

The soldiers left Gino on the ground with the sergeant standing over him. There were only three other rooms in the barracks, including the bathroom. The two soldiers quickly went through the bathroom and the room on the other end of the barracks. After about a minute, a soldier gestured for the major to come see what they found.

Braun grabbed Gino's left arm and neck to lead him into the room ahead of the major. There were shelves full of canned goods, blankets, flour, sugar, tools, and wine.

"Where did you get all this from?" asked the major.

"Most of these items are what was left over from the soldiers shipped out to Russia, but some items we acquired through our work as electricians. Nobody has any money anymore, so they pay us with goods."

The sergeant shoved him to the ground.

"Go check the rest of the barracks for any hidden compartments in the roof or below the floor," Schmidt ordered.

***

Giacomo was running late as usual, but this time it was for a good reason; he had gotten ahold of some great breakfast pastries for a change. Most of the Italian pastry stores had problems getting baking items because of the war effort; it was hit or miss.

As he neared the barracks, he noticed the German vehicles in front.

That can't be good.

Giacomo stopped the truck and quickly made his way to the back of the barracks to hear what was going on inside. He heard a lot of talking. The side window would offer the best view of the entire barracks. He moved toward this viewing platform.

The major was looking at all the goods on the shelves. Giacomo heard the soldiers moving furniture.

"Private, you're telling me all these items are from your dealings with the locals and you haven't been smuggling them up north?"

"Major, we aren't smugglers. We are Italian Royal Army regulars that were wounded, and now we serve our country as electricians here in Rome."

The major gave the sergeant a quick nod.

"Stop lying to the major!" yelled Braun as he ripped into Gino's chin with another right hook.

Gino flew back with such force that his head hit the wall before the rest of his body. He tasted the sudden rush of blood in his mouth and felt it running from his nose. As he looked up, he saw the soldiers through the doorway of the office. They were moving the table hiding the access panel. He shook his head to get his bearings and was reaching into the back of his pants when the sergeant put both hands against the wall and kicked him in the stomach.

The major sat at the table in the middle of the office. He watched Braun kick the private into the fetal position before he opened a bottle of wine.

"Sergeant, stop so he can tell us the truth for once today."

Schmidt found a glass in the top drawer of the desk. The captured private coughed from the beating.

"Sergeant, why don't you take the private over there so we can properly question him," said the major, pointing to the vacant chair in the corner.

Braun leaned down, grabbing a handful of hair with his left hand and wrapping the other arm around Gino's neck. Gino grabbed the sergeant's forearm to release some pressure on his throat and choked on his blood. The sergeant squeezed his right arm tighter as he moved Gino to the chair and pushed him into it. Gino shook his head again to clear it, but this time the room was spinning.

"Okay, now let's see if you can answer the questions," said the major as he sipped the wine.

Giacomo bent down below the last piece of window trim so he wouldn't be detected. As he raised his head to see what was going on in the barracks, a soldier yelled, "Major, we found something underneath the table."

He saw Gino bloodied and sitting on a chair.

He looks like he's seen better days, thought Giacomo as he lowered his head.

He heard a familiar voice—the fat sergeant who had beaten him.

He had dreamed of getting back at the sergeant who gave him the beating of his life. If it wasn't for Gino coming back, Giacomo's corpse would be in that ditch of horror. Now it was his turn to save his friend and, for once, get even for the brutality of these Nazi soldiers.

I need to move now! Giacomo headed back to the truck.

The soldiers yelled from the main room of the barracks. Gino knew they'd found the hidden compartment underneath the table, but all he did was smile through his pain. The major got up and walked into the main room.

"Watch him until I get back. Make sure he doesn't move from the chair!" ordered the major.

"It will be my pleasure, sir," replied Braun, punching Gino in the stomach.

The major made the turn toward the table to see the two soldiers looking down into a hidden access door that was raised. The major went in between the soldiers and got down on his knees to look into the hole, but there was nothing there but dirt and some empty Italian-army-issue food boxes.

"This is all you found?" yelled the major.

"Yes, sir, and we searched the whole barracks."

The major rose as the barracks' main door opened.

Gino heard the door open and reached behind his back with his right hand. The sergeant turned as the Italian giant came in carrying a box of food.

"Is anybody hungry this morning?" asked Giacomo, pulling the trigger of the Beretta hidden in the box.

His first bullet hit the soldier on the major's left in the chest. He fell back against the wall, motionless. The other soldier reached for the rifle leaning on a chair next to him. Giacomo fired his second bullet. This projectile also found its mark and the soldier crumpled.

Braun charged at Giacomo. Gino finally reached his Beretta. The room was still spinning when he stood to help his friend.

The major was waiting for his bullets when the sergeant came out of nowhere and tackled the big Italian to the ground. Schmidt grabbed the German Luger from his holster as the two big men wrestled.

Gino fell through the doorway and saw the sergeant on top of his friend. The major moved toward the two men with his pistol at the ready. Gino aimed at the smug Gestapo officer. The major suddenly turned his Luger on Gino, who fired first, hitting his mark straight in the forehead. The major fell to his knees with his eyes wide open, still holding the Luger.

Giacomo held Braun at bay in case he needed him as a shield, but Gino put that to rest. Giacomo sent Braun flying toward his three fallen comrades with one punch to the face. Gino stood now, and he pointed his Beretta at the sergeant.

"If you move a muscle, I am going to unload this gun into your body!" yelled Gino.

Giacomo grabbed his Beretta from the floor and rose to aim it at Braun.

"How are you doing, Gino?"

"I'm fine."

"You two won't get far before they find you and hang you like all the other Italian rebels. Let me bring you in and I'll tell them the major went crazy," said the sergeant, his hands in the air.

Gino had lost a lot of blood but still had enough energy to hold the gun.

"Do you remember me?" asked Giacomo.

The German was looking at both of them with his hands still in the air.

"Of course I do. You're the electricians that did the work in the ghetto."

Gino and Giacomo glanced at each other before turning their attention back to the shaking German filth.

"What will happen to us when you turn us in?" asked Giacomo.

"You will be sent to a working camp in Germany," replied

the sergeant.

Gino tilted his head from side to side.

"You don't remember what happened in the ditch?" asked Giacomo.

The sergeant looked at Gino for a second and turned his eyes to Giacomo. He finally recognized the big Italian soldier from the past. Braun lunged at Gino. He didn't get far before both Berettas fired. The sergeant's lifeless body lay next to his comrades.

"We need to get out of here," said Giacomo.

It was the last thing Gino heard before he collapsed.

***

Gino could feel the cool air hitting him in his face as they drove with the windows down. He was delirious and one of his eyes was swollen shut, but he could tell he was in the passenger seat of a German sedan. Something felt different as well. Looking down he saw he was wearing a German soldier's uniform. To his left, his partner drove the sedan the major used on a daily basis.

"Where are we going?"

"Go back to sleep, my friend. We're heading someplace safe and out of this crazy army."

Chapter 18

LIEUTENANT MULLER COULDN'T SIT in the major's office at Via Tasso anymore. He had been waiting well over an hour for his mentor. The only information the major's secretary had was that Schmidt received a call from up north and left in his sedan. On a normal day, the lieutenant was supposed to be at the office at around 0800, but he was running late. Without the sedan, Muller couldn't do most of his duties, which today included picking up the major's companion, Hilda.

She was arriving from Berlin to join the major for a week's vacation. The train was arriving late that morning, and he needed some type of transportation. For the major not to be in his office at this time of the day was unusual. There would be no walking for this Gestapo lieutenant, let alone using a bicycle, which was how he traveled to work that morning. There had to be another vehicle available for him to pick up Fraulein Straus.

He decided to see if Sergeant Lucciano knew the location of the major.

He's probably at the ghetto moving people around, thought the lieutenant as he made his way to the Italian colonel's outer office.

"Sergeant, have you seen Major Schmidt today?" asked the lieutenant.

Lucciano, who was doing his daily mundane work, gradually lifted his gaze to the lieutenant and replied, "No. Maybe he's with the colonel."

The sergeant did not have to stand and salute for the lieutenant like he did for the major; in fact, he found the junior officer annoying. Without asking, Lieutenant Muller walked to the colonel's office to see if the major was there. It was empty.

"Colonel Specca is not in his office. He's out," said the sergeant as the lieutenant emerged looking frustrated.

"I need a vehicle to go to the ghetto and pick up the major's guest later this morning. The major might be at the ghetto doing some type of work."

A loud bang suddenly came from the sergeant's desk. The lieutenant took a step back. Slowly, Lucciano rose from his chair holding a set of keys.

"These are the keys to the colonel's sedan. If you so much as put a scratch on it, he will have you for breakfast. Make sure you bring it back before he goes to lunch at one."

The sergeant tossed the keys to the lieutenant, who was already moving out the door to search for Major Schmidt.

Getting to the ghetto was a lot easier with the major's office in Via Tasso. It was only about five kilometers west toward the Tiber River. When the major lived near Vatican City, it was such a long drive that the lieutenant would purposely get lost to avoid going back and forth all day long.

He headed to the major's office, looking down the corridor to check if the colonel's sedan was out front.

"Has he returned yet?" the lieutenant asked Marta, who didn't even look at the bothersome officer.

"No."

After her quick answer, he went to the Italian military sedan. Driving a Fiat 508CM was demeaning for a Gestapo officer, but it was better than walking or riding the bike.

The ghetto was quiet as the lieutenant drove toward the waterfront and train station. He slowed at several points along the way to see if he could spot the major's sedan. He guessed that Major Schmidt might be making routine checks or stopping by the nearby Italian army compounds. There was no sedan in sight. After coming to a stop in the parking spot usually occupied by the troop transport, the lieutenant was met by one of his soldiers. After their usual salutes, he noticed it was the corporal and not Sergeant Braun.

"Where is the sergeant?"

"He and some of the soldiers went with the major, sir."

"Where did they go, and how long have they been gone?" asked the lieutenant.

"Sir, they left about two hours ago and were going to someone's barracks. That is all I know."

Muller immediately knew where the major went. "Grab another soldier and get into the car. We're going to visit our local Italian electricians. Before we head to the barracks, we need to pick up a visitor from the train station."

As the lieutenant pulled the Fiat into the German and Italian headquarters, he saw the Italian colonel yelling at Sergeant Lucciano. He was pointing into his face like he might a child who had misbehaved. Specca turned as the lieutenant pulled up with his car, which seemed to infuriate him even more.

"What should we do, Herr Lieutenant?" asked the corporal in the back seat.

"Nothing. I will handle the colonel. You two need to get out so I can get the major's visitor. Corporal, come with me," ordered the lieutenant.

The corporal quickly opened the passenger door to meet the lieutenant on the other side of the Fiat. Before they were past the Fiat, the sergeant who gave him the keys was nowhere to be found.

"What was the emergency that required you to convince my sergeant to give you my sedan?" asked the colonel.

The lieutenant and corporal exchanged salutes with the colonel before Muller responded.

"Colonel Specca, there is no sign of Major Schmidt or his sedan. My corporal has informed me the major took some soldiers to the old Italian barracks. Now, why did he take soldiers to the barracks? I don't know, but my hunch is there are soldiers involved with smuggling or, worse, some type of revolt."

The colonel crossed his arms to show he wasn't thrilled about this news, especially if it involved Italian soldiers.

"What proof do you have this is true?"

"I don't have any proof right now, but I do know he received a phone call from up north earlier this morning. He left his office in a hurry and hasn't been seen since. I've checked everywhere but the old Italian barracks."

This wasn't anything the colonel hadn't heard before. All his men were involved with some type of smuggling or talking about revolting from the Axis powers.

"Exactly who is in the barracks, and why do they interest the major?"

The lieutenant wasn't too sure what to say at this point because he was already running late to pick up Hilda.

"Colonel, I can't say exactly who he's interested in, but they are workers at the Hotel Roma."

There were only a few soldiers left that worked in the hotel.

"Let's go see if the major has made his way to the barracks," ordered the colonel, going to the Fiat.

"Colonel, I have to pick up a guest of the major's at the train station. If I don't, he will be extremely mad. You can come, and after we drop her off, we can check the barracks."

"Come get me after you drop her off. I want to make sure you get support from us during this operation."

The German soldiers stood at attention as he walked past them, and the lieutenant climbed into the Fiat to pick up Hilda.

***

Hundreds of passengers were inside the train terminal. Most wore Italian or German uniforms, but there were a fair number of civilians, mostly women with children. This wasn't a place to be confused or lost.

A tall, stunning blonde emerged from the lead passenger train holding a suitcase. The conductor immediately rushed forward and offered his assistance in getting down the steps.

"Do you have any other luggage, madam?" asked the conductor.

"Why yes. I have one other bag inside this doorway," answered the German blonde, who was holding her nose to escape the strong smell of coal lingering in the air.

The conductor retrieved her second bag quickly.

"Thank you." She handed him a small coin for his assistance.

After gathering her belongings, the blonde walked to the head of the tracks. This was her second visit to Rome. During her first visit, the Hero of Hannut met her as she exited the train, but not today. As she moved down the concrete peninsula with trains on either side of her, she remembered making a right toward the exit. Hopefully, there would be someone waiting. If not, she would have to take a cab to Via Tasso. There was always the possibility of his being busy, but she was a little upset her major wasn't waiting.

She saw where most of the passengers were exiting the station and quickly followed them, finally emerging into the fresh air. Breathing deeply and exhaling the last of the coal, she scanned her surroundings, looking for a sign that she didn't need a cab.

Lieutenant Muller's trip to the railroad station wasn't far, but with so much going on in Rome, getting close to the entrance was a challenge. Normally, everyone moved out of his way, but that was with the major's sedan. Today he was driving the Italian colonel's Fiat, which commanded little respect or fear. As he was about to abandon the Fiat for a faster pace in his military-issued boots, he noticed Hilda through the crowd blocking the station. She was easy to spot since she was almost as tall as the major. Most Italians barely topped a meter and half, which always made the lieutenant wonder how such little people had once conquered the world.

Hilda looked left and right for anybody or anything she recognized, but nothing caught her eye. She decided to get closer to the road; at least it would be easier for her to get a cab for the short ride to Schmidt's office.

The lieutenant could no longer tolerate the slow-moving traffic. He moved the Fiat as close to the curb as possible and, after shutting down the Italian-made vehicle, he exited the car.

Hilda was about to hold her hand up for a cab when she heard her name.

"Fraulein Straus, it's good to see you again. Major Schmidt is busy this morning and has sent me to get you. He will be meeting you later for lunch," remarked the lieutenant as he bent to take her bags.

"It is good to see you again, Lieutenant, and I know how

busy he can get. His job is his top priority. Where will we be going from here?" asked Hilda as she followed him to the Fiat.

"The major likes to eat right outside of the compound at one of the German bakeries. They serve lunch as well. I will drop you off there until he finishes this morning's business. He might be at the compound right now. We will have to see," replied the lieutenant, reaching for the passenger door. "Let's get you something to eat."

Chapter 19

GIACOMO HEADED FOR THE only place he thought would give them a shot at getting out of this madness—the Hotel Roma. After leaving Rome, he made the last turn into the hotel parking lot near the entrance of the bar. Enrico was outside smoking a cigarette with some of his other workers. As Giacomo slowly approached, the bartender said something and all the other workers went inside. Enrico was the lone person in Giacomo's view as he stopped the car short of the bartender. He exited, glancing at his buddy to make sure he was still breathing.

"We heard there was some shooting at the barracks but didn't realize how bad it was until now," remarked Enrico as he looked into the car to assess Gino's injuries.

Gino's entire body throbbed from the pain. The wind had stopped blowing in his face, which meant the vehicle had stopped. He opened his good eye and noticed he was the only one in the sedan. As he sat up, he saw his giant friend in front of the sedan talking to what looked like the bartender from the Hotel Roma.

"How many did you kill, and did you recognize any of them?" asked Enrico.

Giacomo looked at the bartender for a second, trying to remember how many bodies were in barracks.

"I think it was four or five. It happened so fast I didn't get a chance to count. We did kill Major Schmidt and Sergeant Braun."

The bartender backed away for a second when he heard who they had killed. He turned and considered their situation. The shock had worn off slightly when he turned back to the large Italian, who was dressed in a uniform that wasn't going to fit him anytime soon.

"You both need to leave Rome, now. How injured is Gino?"

"He was beaten pretty bad; he may have some broken ribs, a broken jaw and I think his nose is broken, but it's hard to tell with all the swelling."

"There is a place down south that is safe and will take care of you both. Go to Cassino and find the monastery Monte Cassino. They will take care of Gino and give you a safe place to stay until he is better. I will let them know you're on your way, and you must leave when he is better and head north to join the resistance. They need soldiers like you that aren't afraid of the Germans." Enrico looked toward the door to the bar.

Giacomo looked as well, and another supporter there nodded at Enrico's gesture.

"I'll gather some of my folks and hopefully get to the barracks before anybody else. We need to get rid of those bodies, or the Germans will take revenge on the whole city for the loss of their comrades. They will anyway, but at least we can delay the inevitable. Where is your work truck?"

Giacomo reached into the German uniform's front pocket and handed Enrico a set of keys to the work truck. "It's at the barracks."

Gino was watching his friend, and he smiled and laughed when he noticed that Giacomo had ripped the back of the jacket and the pants were about two inches above his ankles. His period of joy lasted about a second until his mouth erupted in an agony he felt throughout his body. His ribs were either broken or bruised from the kicking he took from Braun, making the fetal position the most comfortable for him. As he drifted back to sleep, he heard the driver's door open but was too weak to speak.

Giacomo wanted to do something for his friend but was

powerless to ease his pain. As he started the sedan, he said, "Don't worry, Gino. We're heading to a safe place where they can patch you up. After we arrive there, we need to ditch this sedan. When you're better, we're heading north to join the resistance and possibly see our families again."

Gino only mustered a slight smile as he drifted back into a painful sleep.

Giacomo watched his friend close his good eye before putting the sedan in gear and lurching forward, off to their safe house at the monastery.

As the German sedan left, Enrico returned to the only home he'd known since the war started—the Hotel Roma.

"Where are the others?" the bartender asked his fellow German haters.

"They're in the back room waiting for your instructions."

"Get the car. We need to clean up a mess at the old Italian barracks. We'll also need some shovels, buckets and mops."

The subordinate made his way to the back room to get things moving. After a few minutes of discussion, the group dispersed.

"They're getting our supplies while I get the car. We'll be back to pick you up."

Enrico headed for the exit, knowing he only had a small window to make his phone call. He only made this call when he was alone, with a number that was held in the highest secrecy. His instructions were to dial the number, wait for four rings, and hang up and dial again. If the phone was answered the second time, then this was his contact to the rebel movement against the German invaders of Rome. After the phone rang four times, he hung up and he dialed again.

"Hello."

The bartender was brief. "This is the Hotel Roma. Is the colonel there?"

***

With Hilda safely in the care of the local German baker, the lieutenant returned to the colonel's office to retrieve the higher-ranking officer. Muller's two soldiers awaited further orders in the breezeway.

"Has the major come back?" asked the lieutenant.

"No sir, he has not, and the Italian colonel is waiting for you in his office."

When Lieutenant Muller strolled into the office, Sergeant Lucciano was still not looking his best.

"Is the colonel in his office?"

Lucciano offered no reply, just a gesture toward the door. Without stopping for what was surely going to be an uncomfortable gathering in the outer office the lieutenant entered the colonel's office. Colonel Specca held up his finger to keep Muller quiet as he finished his phone call.

"Okay, I understand. And how long do you need?" the colonel asked the Hotel Roma bartender.

"I won't know until I get there, but it will be a while to clean that mess. I'll start a fire to signal we have completed the cleanup and that we've left."

"Do the best you can while I figure out what to do on this side of the city. We need to clean this quickly." After hanging up, he looked to the window for some type of answer to this serious problem.

I need to hold the Gestapo here for as long as it will take, he thought.

The lieutenant was already sitting.

"Stay here until I get back," ordered Specca as he left his office and sprinted down the corridor to Major Schmidt's office.

Marta was in her normal position to greet or take requests for her boss when the Italian colonel walked past her.

"Can I help you?"

Before she could get to her feet, Specca was already in the major's office.

"I am going to wait for the major here. Please let me know when he arrives," ordered the colonel, shutting the door behind him.

***

The crew from the hotel pulled into the barracks. Nothing outside indicated any type of physical altercation. Enrico noticed a troop transport and the familiar Italian work truck parked in front. The whole area was still and quiet—too quiet.

"Louie, go see if the keys are in the troop transport. If they are, back it up to the front entrance of the barracks," ordered the bartender.

Louie Costa had joined the group only recently. There was no doubt he was a German hater, but he was always looking for some opportunity for himself, which didn't sit well with the other rebels. Enrico hated using him, but today they needed all available men to complete this clean-up.

As he approached the entrance with a Berretta at the ready, he ordered another sympathizer to stay outside and make sure no one came in while they cleaned whatever carnage awaited them.

This left Enrico and one other sympathizer to go inside. He gestured for his partner to peek through the window on the right while he went to the left one. As he was about to look inside, he jumped at the sound of the truck being started. He smiled a bit—at least they could load the bodies in their own vehicle. Going back to the window, he saw four bodies stacked at the back of the barracks to his right. There was nothing to his left but an empty room with something red on the wall.

The transport was already being backed into position with the help of the sympathizer watching for other visitors.

"Come on. Let's see what we need to get out of here as quickly as possible," Enrico said.

As his partner opened the door, Enrico entered with his Beretta and ducked right to make sure there were no surprises. He determined the only breathing human was him.

"We're clear," called out the leader of the sympathizers.

His partner was already beside him. Holstering his Berretta, Enrico went left to see what secrets were held in that section of the barracks. As he peered around the corner, he saw some much-needed food, wine, and blankets they could all use. He also noticed a broken chair near the entrance and blood all over the wall and floor.

"That is possibly where Mr. Cartelli was beaten," Enrico remarked.

A noise drew their attention to the front entrance of the barracks. Louie stood and stared at the pile of bodies next to the trapdoor.

"Okay, let's get started. Search them for anything we can use.

Take their guns, shoes and uniforms, and load them into the trunk of the car. Load their bodies onto the troop transport as quickly as possible. I am going to load as much of these supplies as we can carry from this storage area. If the Germans find out what happened here, this place will be torched," ordered Enrico.

Louie and the other sympathizer went to the bodies. This first body was a large man already stripped down to his underwear. Louie grabbed the head and shoulders while his partner grabbed the feet.

"This one has a lot of bullet holes in him and is heavy," remarked Louie, grunting his displeasure.

After loading the first soldier, they went back for the next one, who was clearly an officer. He was on his stomach, but Louie could tell he had been shot in the head. Not wanting to see the actual wound unless it was necessary, he unbuttoned the uniform from the back while his partner removed the dead officer's shoes and pants.

"This one is as big as the other one but isn't as fat," remarked Louie as he struggled with the shirt.

As he worked one side of the shirt off the body, he pulled it to the right, but something was holding it around the dead officer's neck. He reached to loosen the black-and-silver ribbon, but it broke off from the clasp and disappeared underneath the other bodies. Louie continued to strip the soldier down without looking for what had fallen from the soldier's uniform. It was of no importance to him.

***

The Italian colonel had to move quickly to ensure no evidence could lead to what happened to the major from his office. As soon as he reached Major Schmidt's desk, he searched every drawer, rifling through every single nook and corner of the immense desk. He found only a few pieces of correspondence that referenced any type of Italian rebellion.

With the speed of a man on a mission, he looked through a file cabinet and removed all documents referencing the Italian resistance or rebellion. The colonel pondered whether to destroy the files or alter them. Surely, the Germans would expect Major Schmidt to have some paperwork on the resistance. That's why he was there.

Specca hated the major and the previous Gestapo watchdog before him. He was personally responsible for having the previous Gestapo colonel transferred but had miscalculated. He thought Schmidt would also be sent away. Major Schmidt made matters worse in the city of Rome, which bothered the Italian Royal Family, who were looking for ways to get out from under control of the Germans and for Italy to exit the war itself.

***

The Gestapo lieutenant became impatient waiting for the Italian colonel to return to his office. He glanced at his watch; it was already fifteen minutes since he left.

Where could have he gone? Something isn't right here, thought Lieutenant Muller, getting up. Major Schmidt was missing, Specca had run off without a word, and there was word of smuggling involving local Italian soldiers.

"Sergeant Lucciano, get me Gestapo headquarters on the phone," ordered the lieutenant.

The sergeant reached for the phone and dialed the local switchboard for an outside line to Germany. Muller stood next to his desk, watching him make progress in his quest for a higher authority's counsel. The sergeant could get through a lot faster than anyone else in this city; the waiting time would be twice as long if anyone else tried to get Germany.

Knowing there was time to spare, the lieutenant went outside to get some fresh air and hopefully see the lanky, lazy Italian running around. As he lit his cigarette and scanned the office complex horizon for his intended target, the door opened. He turned to see the sergeant.

"Lieutenant, I have a Major Fischner from Gestapo headquarters on the phone for you."

Muller tossed his cigarette and followed Lucciano to his desk. The lieutenant grabbed the phone and snapped his fingers, gesturing for the sergeant and secretary to leave so he could talk in private.

The door shut behind the office workers.

"Major, this is Lieutenant Muller from Rome. I believe I have a situation here, and I need some advice."

***

The sergeant smoked his cigarette and looked through the window to see what was going in the office. Lieutenant Muller was nodding and listening intently. Having been pushed out of his office repeatedly in the past, the sergeant knew the call could take a while.

"Are you hungry?" asked Lucciano. Gilda Deluca nodded. "I'll be right back. If the lieutenant asks, tell him I went to get some food." The sergeant threw out the rest of his cigarette before heading to the German bakery around the corner.

At the bakery entrance, the sergeant noticed a woman sitting with a cup of coffee.

"Sergeant, is that you?" asked the major's companion, Hilda. She was dressed in traveling clothes with a suitcase beside her, and she looked like she had already finished her meal.

"Fraulein Straus, it's good to see you again. Are you waiting for Herr Major?" asked the sergeant.

"Yes, I am. I was told that the major is out doing business, so Lieutenant Muller asked me to wait for him while they locate him. Will you please join me for something to eat?"

"Fraulein, it would be my pleasure to join you. I will be right back."

After a five-minute wait, Lucciano emerged from the bakery, hands full of his usual snacks.

"How long have you been waiting for the major?"

"It's been a while, but I understand he is an important man doing great things for our country."

After listening to the extremely beautiful German nurse, Sergeant Lucciano decided to take matters into his own hands. He would deal with the lieutenant's rudeness later.

"How about I grab your bag and let you wait for the major at his office?"

Before he could finish his sentence, Hilda was already standing.

"That would be nice, thank you."

The sergeant grabbed her bag with his free hand and led her toward the compound and a better waiting area.

***

Colonel Specca sat in the chair of the man who'd made his life a miserable nightmare. It was only a matter of time before the pesky German lieutenant waiting in his office showed up asking questions. Specca rose from the comfortable chair and headed for his office but noticed two German soldiers smoking cigarettes at the steps. The nicotine urge took hold of him, and he headed their direction for some relief.

The junior enlisted soldiers instantly came to attention as the senior Italian officer approached them.

"Where is the lieutenant?" asked the colonel, getting a cigarette out of his pocket.

"He's still in your office," answered one of the enlisted.

"Good," responded Colonel Specca as he stepped away from the soldiers so as not to be accused of befriending junior enlisted.

He took the first draw of his cigarette and noticed his sergeant heading toward the major's office with Fraulein Straus. Having only met her briefly during her last visit, he decided not to interfere.

Before the colonel got through the full cigarette, Sergeant Lucciano emerged from the major's office with a rush in his step.

"Taking a food break?" asked the colonel.

The sergeant stopped and saluted his immediate supervisor. "Yes sir; the lieutenant was making a personal call and asked that we leave so he could have some privacy."

"Who did he call?" asked Specca.

"You know, the same people that Major Schmidt is always calling—German headquarters. It seems they call just about every day."

When the sergeant entered the office, the phone was in its resting place and the lieutenant was in the colonel's office. Gilda was already back to her normal, mundane administrative life of filing endless paperwork.

After sitting in the same chair for well over an hour, the German lieutenant had enough. He got up to see what was going on in the outer office. The Gestapo had told him what to do in the event that the colonel had done something to the major.

"Has the colonel come back?" asked Lieutenant Muller.

"No, he has not returned."

"I'm going to look for the colonel," replied the lieutenant as he headed out of the office.

Lucciano looked at Gilda with his usual unconcerned look but curled his upper lip to stress his dislike of the current situation in their office.

Muller saw his intended target ahead, talking to two German soldiers next to the corridor.

"Herr Colonel, I've been waiting for you. When are we leaving?" asked the lieutenant as he approached.

"As soon as I get my hat and make a phone call. I've been told Major Schmidt was last seen at the ghetto. We'll be heading there first," remarked the colonel, proceeding to his office.

"Get your rifles and head to the car," Lieutenant Muller ordered the two soldiers. "I'm going to make sure that lazy Italian officer gets going before the day is done, or I'll have to entertain the major's guest."

The soldiers looked down at their boots with smiles. They grabbed their rifles and headed for the car.

The lieutenant headed for the colonel's office, furious for the delay. He would either be leaving with the colonel or without him, but make no mistake—he was leaving.

Colonel Specca had closed his office door and was about to make a phone call when Lieutenant Muller entered.

"Get your hat; we are leaving now," said the German.

"Herr Lieutenant, have a seat. I need to make a quick phone call, and we'll be leaving for the ghetto."

The German slammed his hand on the receiver and ordered again, "Grab your hat. We are leaving now, or the major will be informed of your actions."

The colonel slowly lowered the phone back down. "There's no reason to get upset. We can leave now. I'll make the call when I get back," answered the colonel, observing the German's right hand on his Luger. "And, Lieutenant, be careful with your belligerence. I'm still the senior officer here."

He rose with caution, never taking his eyes off the German as he gathered his hat and other items.

As they made their way through the outer office, Sergeant Lucciano noticed the lieutenant had his hand on his Luger. He met the lieutenant's eyes and couldn't help but smile as they passed.

Outside, the soldiers stood next to the car awaiting further instructions.

"You two, get in the front; Corporal, you drive," ordered Lieutenant Muller. Without asking where they were going, both soldiers did as they were ordered.

As soon as the soldiers were in the car, the lieutenant ordered, "Head toward the ghetto. If the major is not there, then head straight for the old Italian barracks."

The corporal put the car in reverse and headed for their first destination.

Colonel Specca looked at his watch, noting the time since his call with the Hotel Roma. Well over two hours had passed.

Was that enough time for them to clean up the bodies? he wondered. He wouldn't know for sure until they pulled into the barracks.

Chapter 20

AFTER LOADING THE FOUR bodies on the transport, Louie went back to the barracks and heard a loud splash as Enrico launched a bucket of water at the huge blood puddle.

"We need to get rid of as much blood as possible. Start pushing the water down the trapdoor quickly so we can get out of here. Hopefully, the wooden boards won't stain too much."

Louie grabbed one of the mops and pushed the red water down the trapdoor. He didn't notice the black-and-silver ribbon attached to a metal cross. It floated toward the trapdoor, sliding between the boards.

After countless buckets of water, the room looked like it had been given a bath. Louie set the last chair right next to the table on top of the trapdoor, and he heard the troop transport take off to an unknown destination. He backed out of the barracks, looking in all directions to make sure nothing was out of order. Even Cartelli's blood was a stain no longer visible.

***

As the corporal pulled up to the ghetto compound, Lieutenant Muller was practically in the front seat, peering out the front to see if the major's sedan was in view.

"I don't see the sedan, sir," remarked the corporal.

"Neither do I. Go to the barracks," ordered the Gestapo officer, looking at the Italian colonel.

"Well, I guess he wasn't here after all," remarked Specca as he continued to look for the sedan he knew wouldn't be there.

"Who told you the major was here?"

"My sources are not your concern. They were not wrong, but their timing was off," snapped the colonel.

***

"We ready to get out of here?" asked Enrico.

Louie nodded as he headed for their getaway car. The bartender followed as the fire gathered steam, sending smoke in the air. He looked around the barracks one more time to make sure they didn't leave anything that could link back to the Hotel Roma. Only the work truck was in front of the barracks, which bothered Enrico.

"You go ahead. I'm going to grab the work truck and follow you back to the hotel."

Louie started up the loaded car. With a slight jerk from the engaging clutch, the car headed down the barracks driveway. As Louie turned left toward the hotel, the bartender turned around toward the familiar work truck that had made such a difference to the resistance.

***

The full Fiat headed toward their second stop of the day— one that could be disturbing if the cleanup wasn't successful. The colonel kept watch for any signs of smoke, which would put him at ease. The good news was the Fiat was consistently stopping for pedestrians, livestock, and carts or just about anything the locals could put in the road. Living in this immense city had its drawbacks when it came to driving. The middle of the day wasn't the best time for getting to the barracks outside the city.

"What is taking so long," yelled the lieutenant as he moved from the back seat toward the front to see what the corporal was doing.

"Lieutenant, unless you want me to run over just about anything in our way, we need to stop every so often."

Lieutenant Muller looked out the front window with disgust.

With a hint of a smile, Colonel Specca continued to look for the smoke signal. Gazing at the ancient buildings in this part of the city, he couldn't help but wonder if his countrymen would survive this terrible war. There was no protection from what the Allies or Germans could do to these buildings with their modern bombs, tanks and artillery shells if war came to the city. Surprisingly, he felt tired enough for a quick nap when he heard a gunshot. Muller had taken his Luger out and was shooting in front of the sedan. He looked possessed, shooting with no regard for anyone's safety.

"Herr Lieutenant, put the pistol away before you hurt someone," remarked the Italian colonel. Lieutenant Muller ignored the order and continued to shoot indiscriminately, even toward buildings to show his lack of concern.

"Lieutenant, if you don't put the pistol away, we're going to have a problem in the back seat."

The lieutenant finally looked at the colonel, who was pointing his Berretta at the German's stomach.

"Now, slowly put your pistol away so we can continue our trip without any further hostilities toward my fellow citizens."

The Fiat was at a dead stop in the middle of the cobblestone road laid by the Romans centuries ago. The German soldiers looked in the back seat wondering what to do next.

"But of course, Herr Colonel. How stupid of me to think I could get results through the use of this pistol," responded the lieutenant as he slowly put the Luger back in its holster.

"Why have we stopped? Get this car moving again," ordered Colonel Specca, holstering his pistol as well.

As the colonel was losing hope, he noticed smoke coming from the barracks. Hopefully it wasn't a neighboring farmer cleaning his fields. He left the Berretta unstrapped in case there were any more problems. Even though he was against what the lieutenant did with his pistol, it wasn't uncommon for the Germans to shoot for attention.

***

The work truck roared with the turn of the key. Enrico backed it toward the fire, which was burning at an impressive rate, before heading to the exit and making the left toward Hotel Roma.

"There's something burning up ahead," remarked the corporal.

"There are always fires in this area, especially in the winter months," responded Specca as he looked to see what the driver was talking about.

As he looked toward the brick fence that surrounded the compound, he noticed the familiar work truck drive past them. He quickly looked to see who was driving but only got a glimpse. The colonel was sure that wasn't the normal Italian electrician he had seen so many times getting their work orders. He quickly moved his attention dead ahead of the Fiat. Lieutenant Muller looked out the back window at the work truck.

"Did you see who was driving the truck?" asked the lieutenant.

Nobody responded. The corporal stopped the Fiat before they turned into the compound.

"Do you want me to follow the truck?"

"No, proceed into the compound. I have an idea where they're going. We'll pay them a visit after we find the major."

Both of the officers leaned toward the front seats as they made the right turn into the compound.

"Why do they have a fire going?" asked Lieutenant Muller.

"They're getting rid of some trash, and tonight they may use the fire to heat water for their dinner," answered Colonel Specca. "There are no vehicles here. We must have missed him. He's probably back at the office or somewhere in this vast city. Let's turn around and head back."

"Stop the car. We're going to look around. Everyone get out of the car," ordered the lieutenant.

The two soldiers in front complied with the order, but Specca stayed in the car.

"Let's see what's going on in the barracks," ordered Lieutenant Muller.

"What about the colonel?" asked one of the enlisted.

"Don't worry about him. Go into the barracks and see what's going on. I'll stay here."

The corporal was the first to enter. He looked right and left before heading left to the outer section. The other soldier entered the barracks for his inspection. After a quick look around, the corporal determined that, other than the wet wooden floors, some sleeping bunks, and a table with some chairs, it was pretty much a standard barracks.

The soldiers reported their findings.

"There's nothing in the barracks, except it looks like someone cleaned it because the floor is wet. There are some empty chairs and bunks," responded the corporal. The three men loaded back into the Fiat.

"I suggest we check his residence at Via Tasso, or take me back so I can get some work done," Colonel Specca said.

"Head to the Via Tasso," ordered Lieutenant Muller.

The corporal put the sedan in gear and the lieutenant gave the barracks one last look before they departed. He saw something hanging under the crawl space at the end of the barracks.

"Stop the car," ordered Lieutenant Muller.

He approached the entrance and knelt to get a better look at what was hanging from the barracks floor. It was too far back to see clearly, but whatever it was, he had seen it before. Someone next to him asked, "What is it now?"

The boots next to him were the colonel's.

"There's something hanging under the floor. I'm going to see what it is before we head out."

Before the frustrated Italian could make him change his mind, Muller went to the barracks entrance and looked in the back for the object. The floor was wet, which wasn't unusual. What was odd was that no one seemed to occupy the building. It was empty. *Why mop an empty barracks?* thought the Gestapo lieutenant.

"Where are the personal items of the junior enlisted workers?" he asked as he made his way to the table and chairs at the other end.

"How should I know where their personal items are?" responded the Italian, following.

Lieutenant Muller was looking at the floor when the colonel came up next to him.

"What do you see?" Colonel Specca asked.

"Look how this section of the wood is not wet."

Colonel Specca looked under the table and remarked, "Okay, so what does that mean?" Lieutenant Muller moved the table. Underneath was a perfect, reddish square that wasn't as wet as the surrounding wood.

"Stay here I will be back. Hopefully, I can get these officers to move quicker, so we can get out of here," ordered the corporal as he grabbed his rifle to head back into the barracks.

"Let's see what this door has to offer us." Lieutenant Muller knelt to look for a latch or handle to pull up. There was none, but he managed to get his fingertips inside the outer ridge of the door to open it.

The compartment was empty. He rested his hands on his knees and inspected the whole area before spotting the medal to his right. It was in between the last floorboards.

Colonel Specca slowly grabbed his Berretta to avoid drawing the attention of the kneeling German. As Muller pulled the clasp out of its resting spot, the Italian knew exactly what it was. He'd seen it day after day. He prepared for what was about to happen.

With the steady hand of a man on a mission, Lieutenant Muller guided the metal piece through the cracks of the wood. It was the Iron Cross Major Schmidt wore. Only the major had such an award in Rome. Now it wasn't as bold-looking because of all the blood in the ribbon and metal cross. The German reached for his Luger and heard, "Keep your hands where I can see them and get up slowly." The German did not move.

"Drop you weapon, sir, or I will shoot you," ordered the corporal, pointing his rifle at the colonel. Colonel Specca did as he was ordered. "Put your hands in the air and turn toward me."

Lieutenant Muller rose and grabbed his Luger. With expert speed, he aimed at the back of the Italian's head and pulled the trigger.

He put his Luger back in his holster and walked to the exit, holding the Iron Cross. It was the only evidence that something was corrupt in Rome.

"Leave him here," ordered the lieutenant. He went to the Fiat. "Get in the car. We're leaving."

"Where do you want to go, sir?" asked the corporal.

"Head to the Hotel Roma. I have a feeling all our questions will be answered there."

Chapter 21

ENRICO PULLED INTO THE familiar parking spot Gino and Giacomo used during their time in Rome. As he exited the car, he looked for anything suspicious but noticed nothing. The other supporters were heading in different directions throughout the country. He would be alone in the bar.

The troop transport was on its way to unload the bodies. There would be a mass grave for the fallen soldiers, but no one would lose sleep over their demise. There would be retaliation for what they did, but the longer it took the Germans to figure out what happened, the more time Gino and Giacomo had to escape and the resistance had to prepare.

All the uniforms and supplies recovered from the barracks went north for use by the rebellion. After the bodies were disposed of, the troop transport would also make the trip north. It would have to go by night, using the back roads so as not to be detected.

Enrico made his way back to the bar to continue his undercover work. Before he left for the barracks cleanup, he locked the back door to prevent anybody from entering his domain. Unfortunately, there wasn't any way to close the main entrance to the bar from the hotel lobby. A cautionary glance determined the backroom door remained in the same position as he had left it. It wouldn't be the first time he came back from an errand to find that someone had been looking for something in the bar.

He lowered all the chairs from the tables so the afternoon crowd would have a place to sit. Most patrons would see the chairs on the tables and not even bother to come in. As he finished lowering all of the chairs, he made the familiar turn into the back of the bar.

In the back room, nothing was amiss. He changed into his bartender clothes and went about his daily duties.

***

Lieutenant Muller ordered the corporal to stop well short of the hotel. The long road to the hotel led up a winding hill. The hotel was perfectly placed to see anybody or anything coming well before you pulled in with your car. The lieutenant had frequented the hotel on many occasions and was well aware of how not to be seen.

"Go see if the truck is parked anywhere near the hotel. Stay to the right of the road and close to the woods," he ordered the corporal. "Leave your rifle. Take my pistol in case something isn't right." He handed his Luger to the corporal. "Open the hood of the car. We want to look like the Fiat isn't running."

The corporal slowly ascended the long gravel driveway. As he came to the opening of the narrow road, the immense wooden doors of the Hotel Roma were the first things that came in sight. He veered deeper into the woods. Only a couple of vehicles rested in front of the hotel. None were the work truck. He knelt to make himself more undetectable as he looked to the right of the massive building. It was three stories high with massive pillars. Just about every window was slightly open to allow in air. As he moved toward the hotel, the road opened up to the right. He peered through the bushes, but he only saw a beer sign that read *Carlsberg*, which happened to be the corporal's favorite beer. He decided he'd had enough of the hiding and stood. There in plain view was a newer section of the hotel. It wasn't as tall as the main building but still impressive with its high windows. The windows were not covered; if anybody looked out into the courtyard, he would be seen. The soldier crouched for the final turn. The end of the building came into view and so did the parking lot. He saw the work truck parked at the end next to the woods. That was enough for him.

He backed out of the wooded area to make the short walk back to his superior.

"The work truck is parked at the bar. I saw nobody outside the hotel," reported the corporal as he handed the Luger back.

Lieutenant Muller slammed the hood of the Fiat shut and got in.

"Go to the main entrance," he ordered. "We don't want to spook anybody that might be in the bar. We'll enter from the main lobby. But before we go into the bar, we're going to make a quick phone call."

***

Enrico was doing inventory on the most important items at the bar when he noticed the Fiat roll into the main road and park by the main entrance. Three men exited, a German officer and two enlisted. The three reached the front door and the bellhop was there to greet them.

"Good afternoon, Herr Lieutenant."

Without a word, Lieutenant Muller walked to the front desk. As the bellhop closed the door, he noticed only two visitors where there were three a moment ago.

Enrico saw the soldiers from the bar. One of the enlisted headed to the back entrance. Now he was concerned and needed to make a call before his day ended badly. He dialed the number he used just hours before and would hopefully get the colonel on the line for help.

"Let me see your phone," Lieutenant Muller ordered the front desk clerk.

The clerk handed the phone to the soldier before escaping to the other side of the desk.

Muller dialed Colonel Specca's outer office number. "Sergeant Lucciano, let me know if the colonel's phone is ringing."

"It's ringing right now," answered the sergeant, who was perplexed but always did what he was ordered.

"Answer it," the lieutenant ordered.

"This is Hotel Roma," responded Enrico.

"The colonel is not in his office right now; can I help you?"

Lucciano heard the distinct buzz of the other phone being silenced. He huffed with frustration before heading back to his mundane duties.

After realizing there was no one else to call for help, Enrico hung up. He grabbed his towel and wiped down the bar to look busy for his guests. Before he could look like a bartender with purpose, the door opened from the back, revealing a corporal.

"How can I help you, Herr Corporal?" asked Enrico.

The corporal pointed to the main entrance of the bar. Enrico turned to see what or who was coming into his drinking establishment. It was the lieutenant he had seen here with the colonel and major on several occasions.

"Herr Lieutenant, will the major be joining us or just you three for an early drink?" asked Enrico.

He moved toward the glasses to serve his guest and heard the lieutenant speak.

"Where are the Italian electricians?"

Enrico faced the inquisitive officer.

"What electricians are you talking about? I have been in the bar all day and haven't seen anybody but you so far."

The lieutenant threw something on the bar. Enrico looked down to see Colonel Specca's military hat.

"We know you just tried to call that traitor, Colonel Specca. Now, where are the electricians?" asked Lieutenant Muller, pointing the Luger at Enrico.

Enrico's hands were already up when the corporal moved behind the bar and went into the back room to look around. Nobody said a word. After a few minutes, the corporal emerged with the clothes Enrico had changed out of earlier.

"Why are these clothes wet?" ask the lieutenant, waving them with his free hand.

"Those are the clothes I use to help wash the outside of the hotel. Sitting on a hill, the hotel gets dirty. I don't know what you want from me. I am the only one here and I have never seen that hat before today. The person I called was my distributor. Look, I have my inventory sheets out and I was ordering more alcohol," lied Enrico.

"Come here," ordered the lieutenant.

Enrico did as he was told. As he moved toward the back door, he could tell the situation turned from bad to worse.

"Where are the Italian soldiers that use the truck parked next to your bar?" asked Lieutenant Muller, pointing the gun at Enrico's head.

"That truck has been there all day. They come here to do work on the hotel all the time, but I haven't seen them. When I rode my bike to work this morning, their truck was parked there. Like I said earlier, I am the only one that has been here all day."

The bellhop was reading the newspaper when he heard a loud noise. He raised his head and looked toward the bar. As he got up, through the front windows he saw the three German soldiers walking to their car. The back door was wide open, but there was no sign of Enrico.

"Enrico!" yelled the bellhop. There was no answer, so he walked to the open door and looked down to see Enrico on the ground, motionless.

Chapter 22

THE SUN WAS SETTING when Gino opened his eyes. Without even moving he could tell his body was nowhere near pain-free. Every time he took a breath of fresh air, his chest felt like it would explode. As he lay on the wooden cot, he took account of his surroundings to better assess his predicament.

The sun came in from a lone opening, which was grated with metal rods. The small window was the only source of light. The walls and ceilings were made of granite and stone; so was the floor. As he scanned the rest of the room, Gino noticed a door past his feet. It was open, allowing a cool breeze to flow. There was a small wooden basin near his head—an old wine barrel converted to supply water instead of spirits. A washcloth hung from it. When he tried to stand, the pain immediately intensified. He sat for a moment with his feet resting on the floor. For the first time since the beating, he could open both eyes but not without pain from the side of his head. As he rubbed his head, he felt the large lumps on his skull. There were bandages around his chest and head. The German uniform he had been wearing was in the corner of the room. Other than the bandages, underwear was his only clothing.

Gino slowly rose from the cot but wasn't able to gather enough energy to stand. He did, however, make it to his knees and toward the lone piece of bread and pitcher of water on a table. From the moment he took a bite of the bread, he had a good idea where Giacomo had taken him. This was holy bread, and the white pitcher must be full of holy water. For as long as he could remember, there was only one place which had white pitchers and bread that tasted this way. He was either in a church or some type of monastery. He was about halfway done with the bread and tilting the pitcher for water when he heard a voice.

"Good. You're strong enough to feed yourself."

He looked toward the door and could see a priest standing at the opening with a nun beside him.

"My name is Father Rossi, and this is Sister Caroline," remarked the priest. "Sister, please find Private Cartelli pants and a shirt to wear, or we will have to cut his cot blanket to fit his skinny legs."

The priest came in the room and sat on the edge of the cot. "Looks like you're able to get out of the cot, but I guess standing is an issue."

Gino nodded with embarrassment, figuring he looked ridiculous to the priest. He finished the bread and crawled back to the cot. The priest grabbed him to help him. The priest was strong. Most of the priests Gino had met were either small men or skinny, but this guy was tall and muscular.

"You're still weak and not able to travel, my son. That is fine. You can stay here for as long as you need."

Father Rossi got up and Gino asked, "Where is Giacomo? And where am I?"

Sister Caroline showed up with the clothes.

"Please get our guest more food, and thank you for the clothes," said the priest. He faced Gino. "Don't worry about your friend; he's still here. He'll be joining us later on, but right now you need to eat more and get your strength. You will be busy soon." He placed the clothes on the cot, smiled at the soldier and exited.

Gino was getting ready to change when he looked up to see Sister Caroline with his food. She placed a tray of pasta, bread and cheese next to him. "Will you need help getting dressed?"

Gino blushed. "No thank you, Sister. I can manage myself."

As he ate, voices caught his attention. He pressed his ear against the cold, damp wall.

I need to get out of this room and see who's on the other side of this wall, he thought.

After finishing the meal, Gino dressed. Every movement was excruciating, draining the soldier. Once dressed, he reclined on the cot to sleep and recharge.

***

Sister Caroline was at the fireplace getting dinner ready for Father Rossi and their guests. Giacomo and mountain rebel leader Giuseppe Franco sat at the table with the priest.

"Sister Caroline, please check on our guest to make sure our young soldier doesn't hurt himself."

Giuseppe heard what happened in Rome and quickly left northern Italy to find those responsible. He needed fighters like Giacomo and Gino who knew the German enemy. Most of the freedom fighters were townspeople with little or no fighting experience.

The church was officially neutral on the current war, but in practice it supported local soldiers and despised the Nazis and Italy's Fascist leaders. Even the Italian Royal Family was growing outwardly critical of the situation in Italy.

"Father Rossi, I can't thank you enough for letting us stay here. I know that our being here puts you and the Monte Cassino Monastery at risk with the Germans and Mussolini. As soon as Gino is able to travel, we'll be leaving," said Giacomo.

"The father is doing what he was trained to do, which is to take care of his fellow man. Besides, where are you two going to go? The whole German army is looking for the killers of the Hero of Hannut," said Giuseppe.

"He is right, my son. You wouldn't last long out of these walls. You need to go with Giuseppe up north to join the rebel cause or leave this country. This war will be over in the near future. You both have already seen enough for ten soldiers. It is time to think about your families and break from the enemy."

Giacomo sat looking at the floor. The German uniform was long gone, but not his spirit to fight the Germans. Since they arrived three days ago, the news from Rome got worse. Most of the rebels working at the Hotel Roma had either fled or were killed or captured. Giacomo thought about the Germans who had beaten him. He wanted revenge.

"Your friend is dressed and sleeping. He ate well, too," the nun reported, carrying Gino's empty plate. She carried the German uniform under her arm. Giacomo smiled when she tossed the enemy uniform into the fire.

"Giacomo, we need you and your friend," Giuseppe said. "You know how the Germans operate; besides, you're not afraid of them. The Allies will want to know how to combat the Germans and how they're organized. You saw their operations in Rome firsthand. You know the mood of our Italian soldiers. That could be a big help in ridding this country of those vile Nazis."

Giacomo stood and took a deep breath to speak, but a noise came from the opposite side of the kitchen, from a hidden hallway leading to their room. At a knock, Sister Caroline looked through a hole on the adjacent wall and opened the door for a rebel carrying a submachine gun. He approached Giuseppe and whispered in his ear.

"We have to leave, Giacomo. I will return in two days," Giuseppe said. "Gino needs to heal and ready for the trip north. Will they be safe here, Father Rossi?"

"They will be safe here, my son. Nobody knows about this section of the monastery except for a few that can be trusted. We have used this hiding place for centuries without anybody knowing its location."

"Very well, Father. I need to go. Giacomo, in two days be ready. We won't be coming back after that; it's getting too dangerous down here."

"We will be ready. If I have to carry Gino myself, we're going north. We need to check on our families. When you finally meet Gino, he will let you know how much he hates the Germans. They killed his father, and his two brothers were killed fighting for them."

Giuseppe nodded and shook Giacomo's hand.

As the door closed behind the rebels, Father Rossi said, "I must leave now. There's a service about to start, and if I am not there, people will gossip. Sister Caroline, please get our guests anything they need."

"Thank you, Father," replied Giacomo. Sister Caroline closed the door behind the large priest.

Giacomo went back to eating what was left of his meal as the sister cleaned the dishes left by the previous visitors. After he finished his meal, Giacomo moved toward the open cot located near the hallway entrance that led to Gino's resting place. As he moved his head toward the makeshift pillow, his eyes felt heavy as he watched Sister Caroline go about her business. His thoughts drifted towards his wife and children before he fell into his afternoon slumber.

Giacomo awoke a couple hours later to a familiar face.

"Gino, I see you finally made it out of the room."

"It wasn't easy, but I was hungry and could smell food."

"Are we alone?" asked Giacomo.

"Sister Caroline heard me struggling in the room earlier. She was nice enough to help me out here, but she had to leave. Do you know how hard it is to shut and lock that door?"

"She's probably going to tell Father Rossi you're finally out of their guest room."

Gino laughed but not for long. His one-lunged chest erupted into spasms of pain.

"You alright?" asked Giacomo. He rose from the cot and moved toward the table.

"I'll be fine. The pain is only unbearable when I laugh or take deep breaths. Sergeant Braun did some damage. How long are we going to stay here?"

"We're leaving in two days. The rebels will be back to pick us up. They're planning on taking us north, and hopefully we can visit our families before we get involved with ousting the German scum from this country. Are you going to be ready in two days?"

"Just try and stop me. Besides, if I don't go with you, who's going to watch your back if you get in a jam?" Gino smiled before eating and drinking the wine, which was undoubtedly blessed before its journey down here. They startled at a knock on the door. Giacomo peered through the small wall opening and recognized their visitor: Father Rossi, holding a gunny sack.

"Looks like we're making progress, Private Cartelli," said the priest, walking in with the sack slung over his back.

"I'm not in the army anymore. You can stop calling me private. My first name is Gino, and thank you for all you've done for us. How can we repay you?"

"My sons, this country is going through tough times. We need men like you to get it back on track. You're going to need these when you leave. Which is not in two days but tomorrow." The priest handed the gunny sack to Giacomo. Inside were German Luger and Beretta pistols, clothing and other supplies.

"Looks like the Germans are hunting hard for you two. You've become legends in the resistance, and the Nazis want to make examples of you. I hear they're checking villages, neighborhoods and churches all over. We will need to move you tomorrow. No doubt they'll come snooping around here at some point."

Gino looked at Giacomo and turned his attention to the father. "We know the German army is looking for us, but how do you know about the Germans' manhunt?"

"Our contacts in Rome say it's only a matter of time before the Gestapo place you here. We've already spotted their vehicles coming down south of Rome. Finish eating, my sons; you are going to need your strength for tomorrow. Sister Caroline will be back in the morning. She'll take you to your new hiding place. Make sure you're ready."

Chapter 23

SERGEANT LUCCIANO WAS TIRED of listening to the scuffling noise coming from the German officer's boots as he paced. Lucciano wished his Italian colonel was back, but that wasn't going to happen. Lieutenant Muller moved into the colonel's office and was now in charge. The whole city knew of the massacre at the barracks, including the killing of the Hero of Hannut. And they were shocked to learn that Colonel Specca, the Italian in charge of Rome, aided the resistance by feeding rebels information and covering for them. The Gestapo worried more than ever that their grip on Italy was slipping. The Germans tightened their hold on Rome, sending in more troops to watch over the shifty Italians.

German guards were posted at the entrance of Lieutenant Muller's office. He would soon be promoted as a hero—an example of German cunning and might. Every time Muller left the office he was followed by his new bodyguards. It was the sergeant's job to also protect and control access to him.

A black Mercedes pulled into the parking lot below Muller's window. A corporal emerged and entered the building. Seconds later he was in the foyer requesting to speak to the lieutenant.

"What do you want, Corporal?" asked the sergeant.

"I need to see the lieutenant."

"Go ahead, but make sure you knock."

Lieutenant Muller heard the corporal but pretended he was busy. He didn't want his subordinates to think he was waiting on them. They waited on him. It was a trivial issue, but one taught to him early in his career by his supervisors. He heard the knock.

"Enter," he called out a minute or so after the corporal's knock.

"Lieutenant, I have news about the Italian rebels."

There was a pause as Lieutenant Muller shuffled papers around.

"What is the news?"

"We are not too sure yet, but we have some eyewitnesses who saw the major's car heading out of town toward the Province of Frosinone. We believe the two Italian assassins made their escape in Major Schmidt's sedan."

The lieutenant reached into his top drawer and pulled out a map. He laid it out and stood.

"Show me."

The corporal pointed at the south region of Rome where the car was seen.

"Why would they be going south and not north? Most of the deserters are heading out of the country toward Yugoslavia, not heading south toward more troops." The lieutenant paced, scratching his chin. "I have someone who will follow this lead. He'll be calling me sometime today. Go back to the ghetto, Corporal, until you hear from me. Have at least three other soldiers ready to go south if we hear anything new."

Instead of getting any new insights as to why the deserters would go south, he was thinking about Hilda—the look in her eyes when he told her that her future was destroyed. She was silent when she heard the news; the tears running down her face said plenty. She rose from the chair in his office and asked for a ride to the train station. Nothing was said until they arrived at the station.

"Please let me know if there are any services for the major."

That was the final conversation he had with Hilda Straus. She was a stunningly beautiful woman, indeed, and to watch her so forlorn only agitated the lieutenant further. He wanted to slay the dragon for this beautiful princess.

The phone rang, disrupting the lieutenant's musing about the nurse.

"Lieutenant, you have a call from the Hotel Roma," yelled the sergeant.

He wondered why they called the outer office.

"Have the caller call this number, and close my door," ordered the lieutenant.

With a nod, Lucciano did as he was ordered. As he closed the door, he went to his desk and raised the phone.

"You need to call the lieutenant's personal number. He is waiting for your phone call."

After lowering the receiver, Lucciano grabbed his cigarettes and strutted out for his mid-morning ritual of coffee from the bakery. Gilda Deluca went to the file cabinet next to the lieutenant's door. She was putting files away but, more importantly, also listening to every word that was said.

"What news do you have?" asked the lieutenant.

"Lieutenant, they did leave toward the south. They were last seen about 130 kilometers due south of Rome. We have no other sightings past that point."

The lieutenant looked at his map to see what exactly was located about 130 kilometers from Rome.

The only town at that distance is Cassino, but where in Cassino are they?

Nothing stood out, but he was getting impatient, and so was headquarters. They wanted the killers brought to justice— swiftly and publicly.

"Lieutenant, I have a contact that is looking in the area. I am waiting for a call or message if he finds anything. He has been reliable so far."

"Pay him whatever he wants. I need those two deserters. Give me a call when you hear from him."

The line went dead. Louie Costa put the receiver down and smiled. *No more cleaning floors and tables for me,* he thought. *No more orders from that traitor, Enrico.*

Louie pretended to be an innocent bystander and unwitting accomplish when confronted by the Nazis following the shooting at the barracks. He told them everything he had witnessed— suspicious truck transports, Enrico's secret phone calls, men secretly coming through the hotel's side exits at all hours. The Germans spared him, figuring he was of more use to them as a spy than dead.

After Enrico and the colonel were executed, Louie was offered the job by the hotel manager, but not until he cleaned the Enrico mess. The Germans were able to retrieve most of the uniforms and weapons after Louie transported the items to their headquarters outside Rome. No one suspected he was working for the Germans.

The lieutenant again paced the office. His right hand in his pocket rubbed the Iron Cross once worn by a German hero.

Chapter 24

GINO WAS IN THE fetal position in the single-window room that had been his home for the past four days. He dreamed of Pordenone, and of his lovely Catherina dancing in front of him, without a care in the world. They were both young, without responsibilities, and best of all, there was no war in the dream.

Giacomo wiped his eyes clean of sleep as he entered his friend's room. Sister Caroline had woken him up moments ago.

"We need to get ready to leave. Sister Caroline is already here. There is some food if you want to eat. How is your pain?" Giacomo asked as he put the candleholder down next to the cot.

Gino slowly rose. His pain subsided when he stood.

"It's still there," he said, holding his ribs, "but I can move enough to get out of this place."

Giacomo smiled slightly as he exited.

"Is he able to walk?" asked Sister Caroline.

"He's fine and able to walk. How far do we have to go?"

"We need to walk down the hill into town. Once we get into Cassino, there is a place the church owns that will be your new home until you're picked up tomorrow. We believe you were seen coming to town, but we are not too sure. It's still dark outside, so we need to get going before the sun rises."

"I'm ready," said Gino, joining them. He stepped toward

the table that was their makeshift eating area. As he grabbed some fruit, he noticed the nun wasn't wearing her usual clothes. Instead, she was wearing brown pants, boots, a brown leather jacket, and a white shirt. Her hair was brown and hung midway down her back. She wore some type of holster around her waist. It was all too hard to see with only candlelight.

"Sister, you look different this morning," remarked Gino. He took his first bite of breakfast.

"If I'm dressed like a nun, people will notice me. This way, we blend into the dark. We need to move soon before the sun comes up."

"What about the car?" asked Giacomo.

"We won't need the car. They'll be back today to come get you. Besides, it will give you away quickly. Father Rossi will take care of the car. Get all of your belongings and let's go."

The men looked at each other blankly; they had no personal belongings except for what was in the gunny sack. Giacomo handed Gino his Barretta with the extra ammo.

"We're ready."

Sister Caroline led them through the doorway with a candle in her hand and turned left to leave this section of the monastery. Gino followed the lit candle, his partner directly behind him as they exited the secret room. As Giacomo shut the door, Gino noticed it was hidden behind a religious pennant that stretched the length and width of the door. He turned to find the sister well ahead of him. All he saw was the glowing candle. The ancient walls were full of paintings done centuries before. Most were portraits of people he wondered about only briefly. There was no time to ask who or what the portraits depicted; there was only constant movement toward the exit. They passed many windows about the same size as the one in his room, each window at the same height and evenly spaced. This floor was about six feet below the ground—not the basement but the floor just above. It was dark outside with not even the moon to show their way.

She slowed to let the two deserters catch up with her. They came to a set of steps on the right. She waited until they were right beside her.

"Ready?" she asked.

Both nodded.

"Once we get out in the open, we'll be moving fast. If you can't keep up, let me know and I will slow down," the nun said.

She blew out the candle and knocked on the door three times. The door opened, and the three quickly stepped outside. As soon as they did, the door closed behind them.

Who shut the door? thought Gino.

His eyes adjusted to the darkness and revealed they were in the courtyard. Father Rossi stood next to the door, holding his hand out to Giacomo, who was also adjusting to the darkness.

Father Rossi shook their hands. "Peace be with you, my sons. Sister Caroline will be taking you to a safe place until they come for you. Stay with her and you will be safe; leave her and you will put all of us in jeopardy."

The trio walked down the cobblestone road to the exit.

"Everyone good?" asked the nun. "We're not taking the main road. It's well traveled and will take too long. We're going down the ancient path that only can be traveled by foot or horse."

As he followed their leader, Gino could see the town and its few lights in the distance. The main road curved to the right, and they continued their journey straight. They made their way toward a dirt path leading straight toward the town and the Latin Valley.

The path was heavily wooded, with trees and tall bushes on either side. Most of the path was pitted and uneven from centuries of rain fall. There wasn't much dirt—mostly rocks—under their shoes.

The nun obviously knew the path well, stepping sure-footed and with confidence. Gino felt weak and wobbly on the rocky path; he had trouble keeping up. Most of the journey was downhill, fortunately, better enabling him to keep pace.

The nun stopped abruptly and Gino nearly bumped into her. In front of them was an old man with a small donkey. He did not notice the three travelers while holding the rope reins of his animal companion. The old man and his donkey slowly made their way past them and up the same path, not even stopping to say anything. As they passed out of view, Sister Caroline and the Italian soldiers continued downhill.

"He brings our daily food supply from the village. We don't think he can see anymore. It doesn't matter; the donkey does most of the work and knows the path better than anybody," she said.

They neared the village, the sky lightened, and the path grew wider. Gino had a hard time maneuvering over the last section but managed to not take a tumble as their path turned into cobblestone.

In front of them was the edge of Cassino. Gino smelled evening fires still burning and heard in the distance the cry of a hungry baby. They passed a row of homes that must have been hundreds of years old, each individually landscaped. Some had small stone fences, but most were flush with the road. One had a goat tied in front who couldn't care less about the travelers— until Giacomo stumbled and kicked it. The goat bleated.

"What's going on back there?" the nun admonished.

There was an intersection ahead of them. It was wider than the previous ones, which were more like alleyways than roads. The sister stopped at the last row house on the left. It was on the corner of the intersection and, if you looked out the windows, overlooked all four roads. She slid a large key into the lock. The old door creaked open and the three travelers quickly entered.

"Follow me," the nun said.

They entered another room before the door shut behind them and the sister lit a match, revealing a small storage room.

"Stay here while I make sure we're alone. Sometimes we have unexpected visitors, which would not be in our best interest right now."

Gino saw chairs next to the lit candle she had set down on a small table that was on top of a small rug. He quickly sat to rest, lowering his head so he could breathe a little easier. As he took a deep breath, Giacomo sat beside him.

"I don't know about you, but that was one hell of a hike. My chest is still burning."

Giacomo laughed. "She can move. I was having a hard time keeping up, too. I tripped and kicked that stupid goat."

"I know," said Gino, snickering. "You almost gave us away."

They sat in the light of the candle, not knowing their future. Sounds came from above, which they figured came from Sister

Caroline making sure they were alone. The sounds approached before the door opened, revealing the nun.

"Okay, we're in the clear and the only ones in the house. We'll stay here until my brother picks all of us up."

The Italian soldiers looked at each other before Giacomo said, "Giuseppe is your brother?"

"Yes, he's my brother. By the way, who kicked the goat?"

Chapter 25

LIEUTENANT MULLER ENTERED HIS office as the sun crested. He made his way through the archways and the two guards came to attention and saluted. He returned their salutes before heading into the outer office. As he opened the door, he heard the phone ringing and rushed in to silence the ring. Sergeant Lucciano and Gilda were already at their desks waiting for the day's events to start.

"Hello, this is Lieutenant Muller."

"Lieutenant, the major's car was spotted by some villagers going into the Monte Cassino a few days ago, but it hasn't been seen since. We think the two deserters are hiding in the abbey," replied the spy Louie.

The lieutenant pulled out his map. He already had Monte Cassino circled.

"Good. We're leaving first thing this morning," he said. "Sergeant, grab your hat and assemble my bodyguards. We're going to Monte Cassino. We need to go to the ghetto and grab every German soldier there to come with us."

After they exited, Gilda Deluca slowly rose from her desk to look through the office window. She saw the lieutenant and the other three soldiers get into his sedan. They pulled away from the compound and headed for the ghetto. She grabbed the sergeant's phone and dialed a number she had dialed countless times before. The phone rang a couple of times before someone answered.

"Hello."

"Lieutenant Muller just left and is headed to Monte Cassino."

"Wait a minute," said the person who answered, passing the phone to Giuseppe Franco.

"How many Germans will there be?" asked the Italian rebel.

"I don't know, but he left here with three others. He's going to the ghetto to get the rest of the German soldiers before heading south."

"Thank you." Giuseppe hung up. "We need to leave early and pick up our new recruits in Cassino. Hopefully, we'll get there before the Gestapo."

***

Sunlight came through the bottom of the only access to their storage room.

"You think we could get out of this room?" Gino asked.

"I'm sorry, sure. Let me show you around, but don't look outside. The locals will see you and talk about the new people at the Abbey House. Most of our visitors stay at the monastery, but from time to time we use this place for other reasons. This is one of the other reasons," responded Sister Caroline Franco.

As she opened the door, the sunlight blinded all three occupants momentarily. When their eyes focused, they saw the walls were made of old stones piled neatly in a staggered pattern. The floors were made from smaller cobblestones than were used on the roads. Gino counted three windows, each evenly spaced just like the ones at the monastery. At the top of the stairs was a door.

"This is the basement. It's a left to the front door, which exits to the street adjacent to the one we traveled on last night. If you look out the windows you can see the intersection and all four roads. The main road leading into town is the road next to the front door, Via Monte Cassino. It's used by everyone to get into town and to leave. That's why we used the back entrance last night; it offers less visibility to the nosy locals. Everybody watches this house because of what's going on in the country, so keep low at all times."

Gino and Giacomo stepped back from the outer wall and lowered their heads. Caroline smiled and remarked, "You can relax; all the windows are covered except for the upstairs."

For the first time, Gino noticed Sister Caroline carrying a pistol in her holster. It was smaller than the military issue Gino and Giacomo had carried.

"Where did you get that pistol from?" asked Gino.

"It was my father's during the first war. He died last year, along with all my family members except for Giuseppe. Our father was against this war from the beginning, letting anyone know that cared to listen to him, which was the reason for the raid and his death. Most of the first war veterans are against the war, but they don't vocalize their opinion like our father. We were spared by the Italian Fascists and Germans only because we were not at the house at the time of the raid. After what happened to our family, we decided revenge was the best course of action."

"Are you an actual nun?" asked Giacomo.

"Yes. I was here when they killed my family. Giuseppe visited me to inform me what happened. He didn't ask me to join the rebellion. I asked to join, with the support of Father Rossi. He gives sanctuary to all. The pope has given his blessing to all of us to provide care to anyone who requests it. Let me show you the rest of the house in case you need to get around."

***

They were finally driving south toward their intended target, Monte Cassino. Lieutenant Muller was in the lead vehicle with two troop transports following him. There was a total of ten German soldiers plus the sergeant, who had spent most of the war behind a desk. He looked out of place, but the lieutenant was grateful to have at least one senior enlisted with him.

He had the map in front of him and was looking at the next road. The caravan was on the highway for most of their travel.

"If we don't get lost, we should be there by ten," the lieutenant told Sergeant Lucciano, who was driving the main sedan.

***

Giuseppe neared Cassino in a small car with one other rebel. They came in from the north to avoid detection. If he went on the main road, he would be seen by war supporters. They would tell the Germans and Italian Fascists, and he would be arrested and killed. There was a safe house on the north side of town, with a surprise he learned last year while visiting Caroline.

***

"There it is; take this left," ordered Lieutenant Muller.

Lucciano did as he was ordered, making sure the other two vehicles followed. The lieutenant told him to make another left to Monte Cassio. He looked at the map and gave directions.

"Before we make a left to go up to Monte Cassino, I want you to stop."

This new road was a lot more challenging than the straight highway. It was full of travelers just like Rome. If you tried to avoid a cart or another vehicle, you could end up taking the wrong road.

The German convoy neared the intersection. All the townspeople came outside to see what the noise was about. The sergeant laid on the horn and yelled at the top of his lungs for a clear path for his convoy.

***

Sister Caroline sat in a chair on the main floor, looking into the street through the window. Caroline had changed back into her nun's clothes; she kept an extra set of habits and veils and cassocks at the house for just such an occasion. If anyone saw her through the window, they would only see a nun.

"I am going to step outside and sweep the sidewalk. Don't let anybody in the house until I return," she said.

Gino and Giacomo had taken the chairs out of the storage room and made themselves at home. There wasn't anything to do but sit and wait for whoever was coming to get them. They didn't know there was a race to see who could find them first— Giuseppe or the Gestapo.

Gino stood and put his ear to the wall. He heard the swish of a broom. It wasn't the only noise he heard; there were people walking by, cars moving through the streets and animal bells.

He also heard voices coming from all directions.

"What do you hear?" asked Giacomo.

"A busy town," answered Gino as went back to his chair.

***

Sister Caroline was outside sweeping when she heard the noise coming from Via Monte Cassino. She stopped and saw a Mercedes approaching ahead of a couple of troop transports.

"I want you to stop right at the intersection, where you see the nun sweeping the sidewalk," ordered the lieutenant.

The lieutenant got out of the sedan and waved at the first transport to pass the Mercedes and stop in front of him. He told the driver to block the road ahead.

Gino heard brakes and rumbling and action in the street. Then he heard voices—German voices.

"Germans. They're right outside our building," he whispered to Giacomo.

Giacomo drew his Luger and Gino his Beretta.

As the second transport approached the intersection, Lieutenant Muller raised his hand to stop them.

"I want you to block this intersection with the truck and have your men get out and cover all sides of this intersection until we get back. Let no one leave or enter this road," ordered the German officer.

Sergeant Lucciano was out of the sedan and noticed the nun.

"Which way to Monte Cassino?" he asked Sister Caroline.

She pointed at the road past the troop transport. She continued to sweep the sidewalk but turned toward the front door of the house where her visitors waited for her return.

"Thank you," responded Lucciano as the lieutenant returned from giving orders.

"Let's see what we have up at the Monte Cassino," remarked the lieutenant as the Mercedes leaped into action.

As the transport moved into position, the German soldiers took up stations at each corner.

Sister Caroline turned one last time to assess the situation before going inside. Everyone in the streets took shelter. No one was permitted to enter or leave the block.

Chapter 26

FATHER ROSSI LOOKED DOWN from the hilltop to see what all the clamor was about. These weren't the normal noises he would hear. Most of the time, he ignored what was going on in town, but today wasn't a normal day. He saw the road being blocked and vehicles driving toward the monastery.

"Go ring the bell," the priest ordered the nun standing next to him.

She immediately raced to the courtyard and rang the bell, signaling for everyone to go inside and take cover.

The lieutenant looked up toward the towering walls of Monte Cassino as the ringing started. He knew this was some type of warning signal. The Mercedes turned right into the courtyard just as the bell stopped. Father Rossi stood in the middle of the courtyard waiting for his visitors. The German sedan stopped right in front of the lone priest, who looked fearless with his hands behind his back. As the troop transport entered the courtyard, Lieutenant Muller headed directly for the priest.

"Herr Lieutenant, my name is Father Rossi. How can I help you today?"

The lieutenant looked around before answering. He immediately noticed the major's sedan.

"Where are the soldiers who drove that vehicle here?"

"The two soldiers in German uniforms left yesterday. They needed a place to stay before heading back home. They didn't bother taking the sedan—not too sure why. They may have been deserters. They said they would come back for the car."

"So, priest, you aided deserters?"

"The Roman Catholic Church is not involved with this war and will give sanctuary to whoever wants it. The men wanted to come here to pray. I accommodated them. The pope has given us that direction."

"Sergeant, take the men and search the monastery," ordered Lieutenant Muller.

"Herr Lieutenant, it will take you hours to search this place. It is one of the largest buildings in all of Italy."

"You are right, Father Rossi, and I don't have the time. Sergeant, grab the first nun you see and bring her to me. Have your men search the abbey anyway. If you see anybody in the buildings, send them out to the courtyard."

***

Caroline Franco closed the door to the Abbey House. The deserters were behind the table downstairs, which they turned on its side for cover. Their guns were drawn.

"The Germans are everywhere. They brought a lot of people to look for you. We cannot leave here anytime soon. There are four Germans right outside this door and a transport blocking this intersection. We will have to stay here until Giuseppe shows up."

"He's not going to come here. It's too dangerous," remarked Gino. He went to the wall to listen.

"This will not stop my brother. He has his ways of making a situation work to his advantage," said Sister Caroline, taking off her nun uniform.

Gino was amazed at how easily she transitioned from nun to rebel.

***

It only took about five minutes before the sergeant showed up with the nun who had been ringing the warning bell. The sergeant handed the nun to the lieutenant. Lieutenant Muller grabbed her arm and walked her toward Father Rossi.

"Get on your knees, Sister."

She did as she was told, but not before she placed her hands together and prayed. The German officer pulled out his Luger and aimed at her head.

"Where are the soldiers?" he asked, pointing at the major's sedan.

The priest stepped toward the nun and answered, "I told you before, they left here yesterday. They wanted to go back home and be done with this war."

"Were they alone? And what were they wearing?"

The priest moved closer to the nun but stopped when the lieutenant held up his hand.

"They left with one of my other nuns. She walked them to town. They changed out of their uniforms before they left."

"Were they German or Italian?"

"Does it matter, Herr Lieutenant? We are all God's children."

Lieutenant Muller was getting frustrated but decided to back away. Murdering a nun could have significant consequences and inflame tensions with the Italians. He heard commotion behind him and used it as an excuse to walk away. About fifteen civilians were being kept at bay by the German guards. The guards were watching the German officer harass the priest and nun. Lieutenant Muller holstered his Luger.

"Sergeant, when your men get back from searching the monastery have them line up these bystanders. We might be having a firing squad right here in the courtyard."

Father Rossi overheard the order. He helped the nun to her feet and approached the German.

"Herr Lieutenant, you shouldn't hold these people as prisoners. They had nothing to do with the visitors we had here. I alone let them go with another nun."

The lieutenant stopped walking. His hand in his pocket held the Iron Cross that he carried to remind himself of what happened in Rome. He remembered seeing a nun in the town.

Why was there a nun in the middle of town and not here in the abbey? he thought.

"Father Rossi, why is there a nun in the middle of town sweeping the sidewalk?"

"My nuns provide help to our townspeople who get old. She is caring for one of our elderly citizens."

The lieutenant had enough of the father's answers. Before anyone could guess what was about to happen, the Luger was drawn, and Lieutenant Muller shot Father Rossi in the chest. The lieutenant put the gun to the nun's head again.

"Where are the two soldiers who were here? Are they in town?"

"They left for the Abbey House this morning!" yelled one of the workers in line.

"Where is this Abbey House?" yelled the lieutenant, still holding the gun to her head.

"It's at the last intersection on your right as you come up to the monastery."

"That's where we saw the nun," remarked Lucciano.

"Get in the car," ordered Lieutenant Muller.

As the Mercedes drove away, Sergeant Lucciano looked in the side mirror and saw the nuns kneeling over the father, their hands grasped together, praying for him.

***

Caroline looked at Gino. "Did you hear a gunshot?"

"We need to get out of here or we won't be seeing tomorrow," Giacomo said.

"Sister, get your uniform on and leave this house. If they catch you here, they will kill you, or worse, they will take you prisoner."

"That is my decision to make, and I have made my decision to stay here with you two."

A noise from the storage room alarmed everyone. Gino and Giacomo turned their weapons toward the noise.

"Put your weapons down," the nun said, opening the storage room door.

Giuseppe came in holding a lantern; he hugged his sister.

"You ready to get out of here?"

***

The Mercedes raced down the hill. The transport remained in the same position. The sergeant quickly pulled next to the transport and let out his superior officer.

"Where did the nun go?" asked Lieutenant Muller.

All four of his men looked at him with blank stares; none had seen the nun.

Sergeant Lucciano yelled, "It's this house here, sir!"

The sergeant was already heading for the house with his rifle raised.

"You, grab an axe from the transport and follow me," the lieutenant ordered one of his soldiers.

***

Back in the storage room, the trapdoor was open with the rug hanging over the door. The two deserters had no idea there was a trapdoor at their feet. Sister Caroline was the first to descend the wooden ladder. Giuseppe handed her the lantern.

"Hurry, they'll be coming soon," he said.

Gino was next to go down, followed by Giacomo and last Giuseppe.

Giuseppe grabbed the rope underneath the trapdoor and pulled it closed.

"Hopefully the rug will hide the door. Follow me."

Gino followed the light ahead of him as the four meandered in the darkness As they moved away from the house and into darkness, they heard noise from above.

The sergeant tried to open the door, but it was locked. He moved out of the way and a junior enlisted swung the axe. After the fourth strike at the lock, the door gave way. The sergeant was the first to go in, closely followed by the enlisted. As the lieutenant entered with his Luger at the ready, he could tell they were the only ones in this small house.

"There's no one upstairs," yelled the sergeant.

It was dark and Lieutenant Muller could discern nothing. The junior enlisted poked around a table that was tipped on its side. What little light there was came from covered windows. The lieutenant walked downstairs, moving slowly, before reaching up and pulling the cover off the first window. Something on the ground caught his attention right away—a nun's uniform. He grabbed the uniform with frustration but noticed a door. He moved toward it, flanked by two enlisted. As he opened the door, his men knelt with rifles raised, but there was nothing. Sergeant Lucciano stormed ahead into the room.

"There's nothing here but an old rug," he said.

***

"What are these tunnels?" asked Gino.

"These are the ancient catacombs, we think. There aren't any bodies, but these tunnels were used by the ancient Romans to escape invaders. They're used by the abbey as well," said Giuseppe.

"What's next for us?" asked Gino.

"We're going to the safe house to wait for the Germans to leave. Once they leave, we're going to Lake Como. You'll be able to visit your families for a brief time before we get started on ridding our country of these Germans."

Author Bio

J.R. SHARP'S AWARD-WINNING FIRST book, *Feeding the Enemy*, propelled him into the literary world, and since its release, he has continued sharing his insights on the Italian experience during World War II. He is a retired United States Navy commander who has lived and served all over the world. Visit the author's website at www.jrsharpauthor.com.